Elizabeth Beacon has a passion for history and storytelling—and, with the English West Country on her doorstep, she never lacks a glorious setting for her books. Elizabeth tried horticulture, higher education as a mature student, briefly taught English and worked in an office before finally turning her daydreams about dashing piratical heroes and their stubborn and independent heroines into her dream job: writing Regency romances for Mills & Boon.

Also by Elizabeth Beacon

The Black Sheep's Return
A Wedding for the Scandalous Heiress
A Rake to the Rescue
The Duchess's Secret

The Yelverton Marriages miniseries

Marrying for Love or Money?
Unsuitable Bride for a Viscount

And look out for the next book coming soon!

Discover more at millsandboon.co.uk.

UNSUITABLE BRIDE FOR A VISCOUNT

Elizabeth Beacon

MILLS & BOON

First published in Great Britain 2020
by Mills & Boon, an imprint of HarperCollins*Publishers*
1 London Bridge Street, London, SE1 9GF

Large Print edition 2020

© 2020 Elizabeth Beacon

ISBN: 978-0-263-08652-2

MIX
Paper from
responsible sources
FSC™ C007454

This book is produced from independently certified FSC™ paper to ensure responsible forest management. For more information visit www.harpercollins.co.uk/green.

Printed and bound in Great Britain
by CPI Group (UK) Ltd, Croydon, CR0 4YY

Chapter One

Viscount Stratford hardly noticed the rain-sodden countryside he was riding through or the cloud-veiled hills slowly emerging from the gloom.

Confounded storm, Alaric thought briefly as urgency drove him relentlessly on.

Finding his niece was all that mattered and last night's rain had cost him precious hours. He spent the time pacing a wayside barn impatient for even a glimmer of light and how could he sleep when his niece was missing in a deluge? At this time of year nights were short, and the rain had finally stopped, but at this very moment Juno could be wandering alone and lost and soaked to the skin in the hills—even if she had been taken in by strangers would they be kind to her or use her to make money? He shook his head to try and shake off an image of his naive niece held for ransom by hardy rogues, or lying hurt and feverish somewhere and needing him. So badly it hurt to think that he had failed her yet again.

How had he ever managed to persuade himself it was a good idea to leave Juno in his mother's care while he went to Paris to try and be useful to the Duke of Wellington in his new role as British Ambassador to France? The Royalists and even some former Bonapartists might fawn on the Duke, but it was Bonaparte's former capital, for goodness' sake. It beat Alaric how anyone thought it a good notion to put one of the defeated emperor's foes in such a post, but never mind that now. Juno was all that mattered and thank goodness his London agent had sent warning all was not well so he was already on his way home when she ran away.

And who can blame her when her life was intolerable and you were busy being self-important elsewhere, Stratford? What a fine guardian you have proved to be.

No wonder his orphaned niece had run away to find her former governess, who was now living in the still-sleeping town just visible in the distance. What comfort had Juno ever got from him or his mother?

None at all, the relentless voice of his conscience condemned him once again.

Even thinking about the Dowager Lady Stratford made the weariness of his days on the road between here and Paris lie heavy on his shoulders and he tried to shake it off. But now that Juno had run away from the only family she had left he could not escape the truth any longer. Since he inherited this wretched title he had neglected his niece and driven himself to places he did not really want to go and done things he had no need to do just so he did not have to think about the dratted woman and all the cold places she had left in his life. Which made him a coward, he concluded as he eyed the sleepy Herefordshire town up ahead.

Even if she was not so fond of Miss Grantham, he could see why Juno would set out for this quiet and out-of-the-way place so far from fashionable Mayfair. His mother would sooner walk barefoot down New Bond Street in rags than come here to make her granddaughter return to Stratford House and do as she was bid. So of course Miss Grantham had looked like Juno's best ally in a crisis. The lady had taught, guided and cared for the girl for four years and he had not. His own niece did not feel she could ask him for help when his mother decided to ignore Juno's objections and marry her off against her will to a rich middle-aged peer who was willing to pay the Dowager Lady Stratford handsomely for a young wife and the prospect of an heir as soon as he could get one on her.

'Over my dead body,' Alaric vowed as impatience and guilt made the distance between here and Broadley seem endless.

His horse had to pick its way past ruts and potholes full of floodwater and it would be reckless and cruel to try and spur him on. How dare two selfish aristocrats try to impose such a repellent match on such a young and diffident girl? And what a fool he was to think it would do his shy niece good to meet people her own age who would teach her to take life less seriously. He had only ever wanted her to make a few friends and see that under all the show and sparkle, the polite world was made up of human beings with all the faults, virtues and foibles of their kind. It was never his intention to marry her off so young and especially not against her wishes.

He thought he had made that very clear to his mother when he financed an extravagant new wardrobe for her and Juno and told his staff to make Stratford House ready to launch his niece in style. It was a rite of passage, he had reasoned, an experience Juno would have to go through sooner or later, so she might as well get it out of the way rather than build it up into a dreaded ordeal. And society would expect the only child of the last Viscount Stratford to make her curtsy the moment she was old enough. Alaric did not want whispers there was something wrong with the girl and her family were keeping her close to make her debut seem even more daunting if they put it off until she was older.

He knew Juno was a bright girl who could talk happily enough when she felt at ease with her company because he had heard her laughing and chattering to Miss Grantham on their walks around the park and pleasure gardens at Stratford Park. He even got past her wariness and shyness himself now and again, but they were not close enough to be easy together very often. He had to blame himself for that, as well as so many other things that had gone wrong with Juno's life while he was not looking.

There now, he was on the outskirts of the town he had been aiming for ever since he grimly ordered a fresh horse and set out from Stratford House. At least the place was small enough for him to find the centre easily so he rode his weary and very muddy horse as fast as he dared into the stable yard of the posting inn and tipped a sleepy groom to tend to the animal as it deserved after such stalwart service.

'Do you know of a Milton Cottage?' he asked as the groom yawned, stared sleepily at such a filthy gentleman and scratched his head as if he had never seen the like of him before.

'Aye.'

'Where is it then, man?' Alaric demanded, impatience and terror making him sound harsh. It was either that or fall into the nearest haystack and sleep for a week, but he could not do that until he knew Juno was safe and sound.

'Up yonder.' The man pointed at an area of more prosperous-looking houses to the east of the town and backing on to yet more hills and heath.

'What street?' Alaric demanded, not wanting to waste time wandering about in the sleepy streets looking at every house along the way.

'Hill side of Silver Square—see them little houses almost out of the town by the Big House beyond, governor?' Alaric nodded. 'About in the middle is Milton Cottage.'

'My thanks,' Alaric said and tossed the man another coin before striding off as fast as he could go. The sun was nearly up at last so that would have to do. He could not wait for a respectable hour to find out if Juno was safely with her former governess.

It was hardly a square at all by London or Bath standards. The only house worth a second glance was the large one taking up the whole of the south side of the so-called

square with one row of cottages at a right
angle to it and another one ranged opposite.
The rest was open to the view of the western
plain and he could see a hint of distant hills
and thought it was probably a fine prospect
on a clear day. Today only the odd shaft of
sunlight managed to peer past the hurrying
clouds left over from last night's downpour.
Alaric frowned against the brilliance of one
of those bright rays of light as he knocked
on the highly polished brass knocker loudly
enough to tell whoever was supposed to answer it to get out of bed and do their duty.

He was lifting his hand to do it again and
never mind the respectable ladies sleeping
within who had a right to sleep for several
hours yet, he had to know if Juno had got
here safely. At last he heard movement inside and bolts being drawn back, then a key
turning in the lock. About time, he huffed
to himself, and glared into the narrow crack
of space at the stranger warily peering back
at him.

Alaric blinked to make sure he was not
seeing wonders conjured up by his weary
mind instead of a much plainer truth. No,

she was still there, staring back at him as if he was about the worst thing she could imagine opening a door to at any time of day, let alone this one. Ye gods, what ailed him? He had never been the sort of low and lusty fool to ogle and squeeze the maids whenever he managed to catch one alone in a dark corner. He despised masters who preyed on local girls and left a trail of little bastards and ruined lives behind them. Yet even as he was ordering himself to look away and think why he was here and how urgent it was to find Juno his eyes were eating the woman up as if she was the best thing they had ever seen and they could not get enough of her.

A shaft of that curious sunlight darted into the corridor through an open door behind her and added a shine of gold to her honey-coloured hair. She had eyes of a clear, light blue he refused to call forget-me-not because it would be a cliché and there was nothing weary or shopworn about them. Still, he could not think of a better description, so it would have to do for a worn-out fool like him. It was not as if he was going to write poems to a housemaid, so it hardly mattered what colour he called her fascinating blue gaze. Still, his mind would not let go of the delightful picture of this tall and slender female blinking back at him in the early morning light.

She must have slept in her dark-coloured gown and her hair was tumbling down her back and made him want to reach out and find out for himself if it was as softly full of life and as silkily touchable as the brown-and-gold mass looked from here. Her face was a nearly perfect oval and she had finely cut features and a haughty nose, but it was her mouth—generous and still half-asleep and unwary as if it had not yet caught up with the rest of her—that did the most damage. It drew his gaze like a magnet and made him yearn for things he had no right to yearn for. He tried to dismiss the idea of kissing her unguarded lips properly awake as he wondered how such a definite, determined-looking female managed to take orders and skivvy for her so-called betters. And how *would* it feel to kiss that soft and sleepy mouth until the differences between lord and maidservant faded away and he felt as if he had come home at last to a place he was made for and fitted perfectly.

Stiff and still half-asleep, Marianne Turner was woken by hammering on the door and stumbled to open it before whoever was out there could knock again. On her way here hope won over weariness for a heady moment, then reason told her if this was the lost girl she had a very heavy hand with a door knocker. Marianne sighed with tiredness and disappointment as she drew back the bolts and unlocked the door as quietly as she could. The impatience of whoever was out there had made her fumble, which said a lot about impatience and people who used it as a weapon to get their own way.

'About time,' a deep masculine voice grumbled as soon as she had the door open a cautious few inches to eye up the stranger on the doorstep and shake her head in disbelief. He made it sound as if she was incompetent for not coming sooner when he was being rude and demanding at an outrageous hour of the morning.

'What do you mean by thundering on a lady's door at cockcrow? You will wake up half the street.' She blinked at the unshaven, mud-spattered and very male idiot standing on the doorstep as if he had every right to go where he chose and wake up anyone he wanted to and never mind the time. She glared at him and, goodness, there was an awful lot of him to glare at, wasn't there? 'You must have heard me trying to get the door open—have you no manners at all?' she demanded.

'Not with incompetent bunglers. Now hurry up and let me in, then go and tell Miss Grantham I need to speak to her,' he demanded as if she should scurry about at his bidding and curtsy as if her life depended on it all the while and she was not doing that either.

'No,' Marianne said grumpily and refused to be awed by his height and powerful build.

Luckily, he could have no idea Fliss Grantham was not upstairs fast asleep in her maidenly bed. In fact, Fliss had been marooned up in the Broadley Hills by last night's storm and at least Miss Donne's maid had told Marianne's brother, Darius, about a shepherds' hut up there where they could take shelter from the deluge. Secretly Marianne had been delighted that the stubborn pair would now have to admit the powerful attraction between them that had been so obvious from the start. They would have to marry after a night alone in the hills so that was one reason to be cheerful this morning, now she came to think of it. Except this ill-mannered, unshaven and travel-worn stranger had thrust his very muddy boot in the door while she was busy thinking about Fliss and Darius, so now she could not slam it in his face.

Oh, and Fliss's former pupil, Juno Defford, was still missing after a night of heavy rain. She had far more important things to do than wonder how it might feel if this arrogantly masculine fool was clean, had shaved and was as fascinated by her as she was in danger of being by him, if she did not wake up properly and get back to real life.

'Go away and take a bath and shave, then come back at a civilised hour,' she ordered the man impatiently. 'But only if you intend to ask civil questions when you get here, mind. Throwing demands about as if the rest of us cannot wait to obey you sets people's backs up and we have enough to worry about already.'

She glared down at his intrusive foot in the hope he would remove it. No such luck; the man had neither manners nor regard for a lady's peace and privacy. She tried not to blink in the face of his eagle-eyed scrutiny, but he was tall and she was not used to looking up that far at a man. It felt as if a force of nature was glowering back at her and it was far too early in the morning to deal with one of those when she had so many other things to worry about. She eyed the powerful masculine form under his dirt-spattered and travel-worn clothing and wrinkled her nose fastidiously to tell him what she thought of his disreputable state.

Behind several days' growth of beard his features were clean-cut and patrician and she supposed he would look stern and impatient even without the whiskers. With them he looked like a pirate, or a very dirty duellist who was all hard eyes and dangerous edges. Something deep inside her whispered he looked like a warrior rather than the idle gentleman of means his accent and the quality of his clothes under all that dirt argued he must be. She almost preferred him this way if he had to be here at all. The set of smooth-shaven and immaculate gentlemen of fashion he probably belonged to when he was clean and decent and not trying to intimidate his way into strange houses made her inner radical stir and shake her fist at the luxury they took for granted while so many people in this unfair world had nothing but the rags on their backs.

'I must speak with Miss Grantham immediately,' he argued like a king in disguise.

A pretty heavy disguise, she argued silently and stayed where she was.

'On personal business,' he added in the deep and growling voice that secretly sent a shiver of awareness down her spine. 'Kindly let me in without more ado, then go and tell Miss Grantham I have arrived. Never mind if she is dressed or no, it is urgent,' he added as if his outrageous demand would remove her from his path like magic.

'Absolutely not,' she replied, folding her

arms across her body to make it very clear she was going nowhere.

She could stand here until half the towns-folk were wide awake if she had to and she had no intention of telling this grim and arrogant stranger that Fliss had been out all night with a man she would now have to marry if she wanted to save her good name. Even if Marianne had wanted to tell him that tale, it was not hers to tell. The man glared at her again and looked determined to stay in the way until he got what he wanted. She felt a treacherous stir of pity for the dark shadows under his hard blue eyes and the lines of exhaustion so stark around his mouth. He looked as if he had been screwing up his face against the elements and physical weariness most of the way here. He was not wet enough to have been out in the worst of the storm, but he did not look as if he'd spent much of last night sleeping either. In fact he looked as if he had spent days of hard effort and not much sleep to get here with the dawn.

For a fleeting moment he reminded her sharply of her husband Daniel after too many hard days on the march. But this was not the time to weaken or grieve for what she had lost and this man did not need her pity. Her memory of how exhausted she had felt after days in the tail of the Peninsular Army would not help her be sternly objective about him either. And this bossy autocrat had nothing in common with gallant and kind Sergeant Daniel Turner and his beloved but sometimes very weary wife. She reminded herself this man's filthy clothes had once been of the finest quality and no amount of money could buy him a right to stand on a lady's doorstep issuing brusque orders at dawn. He needed taking down a peg or two if he thought it should.

'Go to the local inn and get some sleep,' she told him brusquely. 'If you fall down on their doorstep, at least the grooms and ostlers can carry you to the barn to sleep off your journey. If you collapse out there, we will just have to leave you lying there until you wake up again.'

'I dare say you think you are a good girl protecting your employer's privacy, but a young woman's life could depend on you doing as you are bid, my girl, and you are confoundedly in the way,' he informed her with exaggerated patience, as if she was the last straw he was trying hard not to sweep aside like an annoying fly.

'I am not the maid, you stupid man. Nor am I a girl,' she told him with a sneaky little worm of temper writhing away inside her. He must have taken one look at her slept-in clothes and unkempt hair and decided she was of no account.

'Who are you, then?' he barked impatiently.

'A friend of Miss Grantham's and of her own former governess, Miss Donne—whose privacy you are violating by calling at her house at such an unearthly hour and demanding the company of a lady living under her roof.'

'Privacy be damned,' he said with an exasperated sigh, as if he was still thinking of pushing past her to rouse the household and maybe even opening every door he came across until he found Fliss behind one of them. And all he would find was an empty room and neatly made bed so she could not allow that.

'Do tell me where you live, sir, so I can

organise an early morning invasion of your house and see how *you* like it,' she said and did her best not to blink when he stared back as if daring her to do her worst.

'Stratford Park,' he snapped impatiently.

Oh, no, he must be Viscount Stratford, then—Juno Defford's uncle and guardian and Fliss's former employer. How could she not have realised he was the only autocrat likely to turn up in Broadley demanding Fliss's presence at this ridiculous hour of the day and throwing his weight about when she did not jump to obey his orders? He was supposed to be in Paris annoying the French, but here he was on Miss Donne's doorstep, annoying Marianne instead.

'So *you* are the idiot who caused this unholy mess in the first place,' she said with a glare to let him know what she thought of him for neglecting a girl he should be honour bound to care for.

'Maybe,' he said wearily. He took off a fine and filthy riding glove to rub a hand over his eyes.

'I suppose you really are Lord Stratford?'

she said with haughtily raised brows to let him know his title cut no ice with her.

'Yes, and you are still in my way. Whoever you are, you seem to know a great deal about me and mine although we have never set eyes on one another until this very moment, so you must also know how urgent my mission is and I must suppose you are being rude and obstructive on purpose.'

'Think what you please, I am not rousing the household when they had so little sleep and so much worry yesterday because of what you did to your unfortunate ward.'

'Is Juno here, then—is she safe?'

Chapter Two

At last, there was a gruff but almost painful anxiety for the lost girl in his voice and Marianne had been accusing him of not caring about her ever since she heard Juno Defford's sad story from a panicked Fliss yesterday morning. He had treated the poor child like an unwanted package he could hand over to his mother to be rid of however she chose and look how the wretched woman had chosen to do it. The very idea of such an April and December marriage for the girl had made *her* shudder with revulsion, so goodness knew how alone and desperate such a young woman must have felt when she realised what was being planned for her. Taking a deeper breath to calm her temper and trying to remind herself there were two sides to every story, Marianne struggled to be fair to him, although it really was a struggle.

'No,' she said starkly. She could not give him false hope. There had been no sign of the girl yesterday and no late-night knock on the door to usher in a soaked and exhausted Juno.

'God help us, then,' he murmured wearily, as if hope his ward was here was all that had kept him riding on for what looked like days and the loss of it meant he might collapse after all. 'What must I do to find her?' he added despairingly.

Marianne knew he was not speaking to her when he shut his eyes and swayed as if her *No* was a felling blow. She watched him battle exhaustion and despair and her temper calmed at such signs he really did care about that lonely little rich girl whose only refuge in a storm was her former governess, but something told her sympathy would only revolt such a proud man so she had best not risk it for both their sakes.

'We looked all the way from here to Worcester yesterday and searched every hiding place we could think of on the way back,' she explained curtly. 'The rain was so heavy in the end we could only see a few steps in front of us, so we were forced to give up the search for the night. It will begin again as soon as all the searchers are awake after their long and weary day yesterday.'

'I would not have stopped,' he muttered almost accusingly.

She felt fury flare again and was glad it stopped her having to feel sorry for his lordly arrogance. 'Then you would be no use to anyone now, would you? I told you we could not see for the force of the rain. If you had been out looking for her in it with no idea of the local terrain, we would now be put to the trouble of rescuing you as well as finding your niece.'

'You were out in it as well, then?' he asked incredulously.

'Of course I was. Did you expect me to sit at home sewing while a young woman was lost and alone and with all that brooding cloud about to warn us that a heavy storm was on the way?'

'I expect nothing, ma'am. You are a stranger to me and still in my way.'

His hard expression and stony look of indifference made her temper flare, hot and invigorating this time, and there was no reason to hold back now he had made it so obvious her opinion did not matter a jot. 'Then *expect* me to be furious about a girl's lonely and probably terrifying journey from London to Worcester on the stage. She must have been easy prey for a petty thief and thank God she met with nothing worse than robbery, unschooled as she must be in the ways of rogues and con men. I dare say she has never even travelled by post before, let alone on a public stagecoach, and I admire her for getting as far as she did.

'So you can *expect* me to admire her courage in walking into an unfamiliar countryside when all her money was stolen and I doubt she is used to much more than a leisurely stroll in the Park. And *expect* me to pity a lonely, put-upon girl who felt the only person she could flee to for protection was her former governess. But please *don't* expect me to think *you* care a snap of your fingers for your niece and ward, my lord. I cannot believe you can possibly do so when you left her so alone and friendless under your noble

London roof that she felt she had to come all this way on her own to find sanctuary with the one person who would love and support her come what may.'

'I expect nothing of you. I do not even know who you are,' he replied shortly.

She might have felt her temper hitch even higher if not for the flat weariness in his blue eyes as he stared back at her as if he could hardly see who she was for utter weariness and worry. 'Just as well,' she said grumpily because she did not want to feel compassion for him. Loathing for the haughty and indifferent family who gave a shy girl no choice but to run away from home had powered her through anxiety, fatigue and the threatening storm all day yesterday. She did not want to be fair to him until Juno Defford was safe and she was still very tired herself. She had fallen asleep waiting up for Juno to knock on Miss Donne's door and walk in out of the endless rain. Obviously she needed to be angry with someone to keep on doing whatever had to be done to find the missing girl and he would do very well.

'Who is it, Marianne?' Miss Donne's sleepy

voice demanded from the top of the stairs and Marianne could hear the painful anxiety in it.

Lord Stratford used the momentary distraction to move her out of his way as if she weighed nothing. He was inside the house before she could protest or counter his sneaky move. Oh, drat the man! She cursed him under her breath. She should never have lowered her guard for even a second and now he was sure to get in the way of the search for his niece. He would throw orders out left, right and centre and he had no idea of the shape of the countryside or any of the places where a girl might seek shelter from a storm. Marianne shut the door behind him with an outraged sniff and glared at his lordly back. She had been right about his arrogance and bad manners all along then. How stupid of her to feel even an iota of pity for the man when he obviously did not deserve any.

'Viscount Stratford,' she called out to warn Miss Donne exactly who had broken into her house at an outrageous hour of the morning. Yet her shoulders still felt the echo of his leashed strength under that fleeting touch. She refused to let that be because awareness of him as a man had shot through her when he put her aside as if she was weightless.

'Oh.' Miss Donne's voice gave away her horror at such a visitor arriving at her door at dawn with Fliss not here to greet him.

A few moments of tense silence stretched out and Marianne hoped His Lordship was squirming with discomfort as the wrongness of forcing his way into a lady's residence at such a ridiculous hour of the day finally hit home. No, of course he was not, she decided as his impatient frown stayed firmly in place. He was not capable of examining his own actions and could only pick holes in all they had done yesterday to find his unfortunate niece.

'Then of course you must let His Lordship in, Marianne, dear. Ask him to wait in the front parlour while I dress. I will come down and explain what little we know of his niece's movements as soon as I am fit to be seen.'

Miss Donne's voice faded as she went back to her room and shut the door behind her and Marianne was left eyeing the filthy viscount dubiously. She raised an eyebrow to tell him he was not fit for a lady's parlour, particularly not one as neat and clean as Miss Donne's. 'You could always come back when you are cleaner and more civilised and in a better temper,' she suggested coldly.

'Where is the kitchen?' he barked as if she had not spoken.

'Of course, silly me. You are not humble or polite enough to go away to bathe, shave and change out of your riding clothes and come back later, are you? How could I be so stupid as to think you might act like a gentleman instead of an aristocrat?' she carped as he shot her an impatient glance, then strode down the corridor leading to the cheerful best kitchen Miss Donne and Fliss used as a dining and sitting room when they did not have company. She had left the door open when she stumbled towards the front door still half-asleep to stop his rattle on the front door. Silly of her, she reflected now, as he spotted the obvious place for a filthy and travel-worn gentleman and Marianne had to tag on behind like a sheepdog keeping a wary eye on a fox.

'All I care about is my niece, everything else can wait,' he told her and looked around

the sunny room as if they might be hiding
Juno in a corner.

Now she had to admit to herself he really was desperate to find his niece and he
seemed so much safer when she could fool
herself he was heartless. He sighed when he
realised he was wrong about Juno perhaps
being hidden in here from the likes of him,
then he frowned down at the last faint glow
of last night's fire as if he had never seen
one before. That traitor pity for his desperate state of mind and body turned her heart
over; followed by embarrassment when she
realised her own nest of cushions and covers
was still lying on a Windsor chair like a dis-
carded shell and betraying her own largely
sleepless night.

She hastily folded the quilt Miss Donne's
maid had found for her when Marianne insisted on waiting up just in case the missing
girl found her way to Miss Donne's house
despite the downpour and nobody heard her
knocking. She might as well have accepted
the guest bedroom Miss Donne offered her.
Then at least she would not have woken with
a crick in her neck and half her wits miss-

ing when this man hammered on the front door and startled her out of the rest of them. Marianne plumped up the cushions that had shaped themselves around her while she slept and would have knelt to rekindle the dying fire if he had not got there first.

Silence stretched between them like fine wire this time as he concentrated on reviving the fire and ignored her as best he could. Who would have thought he even knew how, let alone be considerate enough to sweep up the cold ashes on the stone slab to save them spilling out into the room? He looked at the brass shovel full of them when he had gathered them as neatly as he could as if he did not know what to do with them. She was glad of something to look disapproving about as she took it off him without a word, then went outside to add them to the neat ash pile by the back-garden gate. She paused out in the fresh air to frown at a new pall of cloud trying to blot out the early morning sun.

'I really hope it is not going to rain again,' she observed as she re-entered the room. He seemed taller and darker without the sun to lighten the place with a little hope.

He frowned as if it might be her fault it had gone in. 'Where the devil can Juno be?' he barked and glared at her as if she should know. Apparently their brief truce was over now he had got the fire burning nicely and Miss Donne would be down shortly for him to be a lot more polite to.

'If I knew that I would not have been out looking for her most of yesterday,' Marianne snapped because she had only had a couple of hours' uneasy sleep as well and she did not see why she should play the perfect lady when he was being such a poor gentleman.

'If you truly want to help my ward, then tell me everything you know about her journey and the search so far.'

'I doubt if I know much more than you do.'

'All I know is my ward has been missing in the wilds of Herefordshire for far too long. I rode to Worcester, expecting to find out she had taken the Leominster stage to get here at last only to discover some cur took every penny she had so she could not buy a seat. If only I had got to her a few hours earlier I could have saved her the ordeal of wandering penniless and alone through a strange countryside. If only I had left Paris even a day before I did I could have made sure she got here safe and well or that she need not flee in the first place. Because I failed to find her in time my niece is probably lost and frightened half out of her wits at this very moment and even if she has not fallen into the hands of a villain she could be soaked to the skin and in a high fever.'

She had wanted him to show some sign of emotion and now he had she was not quite sure she knew what to do with it all. 'Stop imagining the worst,' she told him briskly. 'For either of us to be of any use in this search we must believe your niece had the good sense to find shelter last night. After having her pocket picked she is sure to be wary of being seen walking alone, so even not finding sight or sound of her is a good thing when you think about it rationally.'

'Where is she, then?' he asked starkly.

All she could do was shake her head in reply because she was tired as well and the girl had seemed to vanish from the face of the earth from the moment she walked across the New Bridge at Worcester and out into the countryside. It was probably as well brisk footsteps on the stone-flagged floor announced Miss Donne's arrival and stopped them both imagining Juno in all sorts of terrible situations now he had put them back into her head.

'Have you brought us good news of Miss Defford, my lord?' Miss Donne asked rather breathlessly.

Marianne marvelled hope could blind such a shrewd lady to Lord Stratford's grim expression and weary eyes.

'Only that she is still lost, ma'am. I hoped to find my niece when I got here and I was bitterly disappointed,' he said wearily.

'Indeed?' Miss Donne said with a sigh as if a heavy weight was back on her shoulders. 'Then we must begin searching once again,' she said resolutely and looked at Marianne as if she would know where to start.

'Miss Defford may be walking into town after sheltering from the storm as we speak,' she made herself say bracingly.

Chapter Three

Alaric stared down at the fire and tried to do as Marianne said and put the worst of his terrors out of his head. He could not call her anything else because he had no idea who she was and where she fitted into brisk little Miss Donne's household and perhaps Miss Grantham's life as well. Speaking of whom, where the devil was the woman? He glared at the door between this cosy room and the rest of the oddly silent and empty-feeling house and sensed yet another mystery on the other side of it. A pity his brain seemed so slow and dazed with lack of sleep since he really needed it smartly aware and on parade with its buttons polished and boots blacked.

It was lack of sleep that made him puzzled and foggy about the unfamiliar new world he seemed to have been wandering in ever since he had reached Stratford House—however long ago that now was—and found out Juno was missing. He would probably find a genuine housemaid, dazzling and quick-witted and even a little bit compassionate towards such a bumbling idiot right now. And wholly delicious and so very unconscious of her own attractions. Tall and slender and just the right height for a lofty lord like him as well, his inner idiot pointed out as he tried to pretend he was as unaware of her as a woman as she seemed of him as a man.

Marianne seemed to be doing her best to pretend he was not even here as she bent cautiously to push the already-filled kettle hanging on its iron arm over the fire without coming anywhere near him. She swiftly stepped back and away as if he might be contagious and he knew he was filthy and smelt of horse and mud and whatever had been in the barn before he took shelter in it last night. He was lucky both ladies had much better manners or a lot more compassion than his mother.

He only had to imagine the Dowager Lady Stratford's hard grey eyes icing over with contempt at even a glimpse, or a whiff, of him right now and he felt all the coldness of his childhood at his back like a January wind from the Arctic ice caps. Shivering in his boots despite the fire and the calendar telling them it was high summer, he tried to gauge whatever it was they were being so careful not to tell him about Miss Grantham's prolonged absence.

He had told himself all the way to Paris and back it was sensible for him to marry kind, well-bred and beautiful Miss Grantham so he could provide a much better home for Juno and a loving mother to his children when they came along. At least he knew enough about bleak and unloving childhoods to want better for his sons and daughters than the one he endured. Yet now he was here and Miss Grantham might have decided to accept his sensible offer of marriage, he felt as if he had left something crucial out of his calculations. Surely he could not have felt as if Marianne was all the warmth and impulsiveness and loyalty he had ever wanted at first glance if there was any more than polite friendship between him and Juno's former governess?

How could he have thought common interests and civility were enough, that instant of surprised and horrified recognition had whispered, as he had stared at a very different female when she had opened the door? He wanted her until his bones ached and a lot more besides he had best not even think about now.

'Tea, my lord?' Miss Donne asked and it felt as if he had to come a long way back to the now sunny-again kitchen to look at her as if he had never even heard of the stuff.

'Hmm?' he heard himself say like a looby.

'A beverage made with leaves from the tea plant and imported from China at great expense,' Marianne pointed out impatiently and with a wave at the fat brown kitchen teapot on the scrubbed table as if he might not have seen one before.

'I do vaguely recall the idea,' he said with a smile of apology for Miss Donne and a wary glance at Marianne in case she had any idea why he had been lost in his thoughts. From the frown of impatience knitting her slender honey-and-brown brows almost together, he imagined to her he was just being an annoying sort of lord again instead of a lustful and predatory one. So at least he had been excused the shame and indignity of being rejected by Marianne Whoever-She-Was before he could do more than stare at her like a mooncalf. That was one horror to cross off his list, then. He did not know if he could face another furious lady telling him how hateful he was and how bitterly she wished he had never been born after his mother did just that when he found out what she had done to Juno and challenged her selfishness and lack of feeling. 'The French seem to prefer coffee,' he added, 'or drink chocolate at breakfast time.'

'You can hardly expect us to roast and grind coffee beans or ask our closest wealthy neighbour to lend us cocoa beans and her chocolate pot when you have turned up on the doorstep with the dawn uninvited, Lord Stratford.'

'Now then, Marianne, that is hardly polite and invitations are unimportant at a time of crisis,' Miss Donne said and Alaric could have hugged her, except he liked her too much already to engulf her in the reek of sweaty man and the less savoury smells of the road.

'Thank you, Miss Donne. Miss...' he let his voice tail off because he could hardly call her Marianne.

'Mrs,' she snapped crossly, and he suspected her tiredness was almost as huge as his when she seemed to repent her brusque impatience with a sigh. 'My name is Mrs Turner,' she admitted as she avoided both their gazes and poured tea into all three breakfast teacups without waiting for any more foolish arguments from him.

Just as well since jealousy and acute hatred of the lucky Mr Turner shot through him in a hot arrow of frustration. He was too late, he let himself mourn silently as the absurdity of being too late for a woman he had not even met an hour ago tried to snap him back to sanity. She obviously did not like him, so that made his feral longing for another man's wife feel even worse.

'I am a widow,' she told him almost defiantly and with no idea she had just freed him from a fire he had never wanted to burn on. He did not have to want another man's wife so unmercifully he was having trouble keeping hold of the elusive thread of this not quite a conversation as well as his dignity.

'I am sorry for your loss,' he lied.

'Thank you,' she said as if that was the last she wanted to hear on the subject. 'Do not let your tea get cold,' she advised him. 'It might not be coffee or chocolate, but it is hot and you look as if you need reviving, my lord.'

'Well, really, my dear,' Miss Donne chided, as if personal comments mattered at a time like this, 'this is not the time for picking at one another with Miss Defford still to find and time a-wasting.'

'No, you are right,' Mrs Turner admitted. 'We need to eat and be out and ready for the search as soon as the others are awake,' she added.

Alaric could only nod his agreement and drink his tea. Both ladies were right, they did need to eat and drink so they would have strength for the resumed search for Juno. His niece was all that mattered and never mind his foolish obsession with a honey-haired widow with dreamy blue eyes and a mouth a man would ride a hundred miles to kiss, if only those eyes were dreamy for him and her mouth half-asleep still after a night of hot and heady loving in his bed.

When Miss Donne's Bet came downstairs, tying her apron and struggling with her cap, she blurted out the story of Fliss walking off into the hills in the pouring rain last night to look for Miss Defford before she even noticed the travel-worn lord lurking in front of the kitchen fire. So then Miss Donne had to tell His Lordship Marianne's brother, Darius, had gone after Fliss and neither of them had returned yet. Lord Stratford had tersely demanded directions and marched out of the back door as soon as Bet could gasp them out. By the time Marianne put her damp shoes on and stumbled after him, the viscount was almost out of sight and obviously in a fine temper. She had been forced to pant after him up the winding lane out of town and even then she only just managed to keep him in sight.

She scurried into earshot just in time to hear why he was in such a hurry. Apparently Darius had compromised Fliss before Lord Stratford could marry her himself. From the dreamy way Fliss was looking at Darius, Lord Stratford would not have got his way even if he had got here in time to keep them apart last night. Then the viscount said Fliss had recently inherited a fortune and accused Darius of being a fortune hunter. How ironic when Darius had tried so hard to resist his attraction to Fliss because she was a poor governess and he thought he should marry money. If Juno's disappearance was not so sharp in all their minds, Marianne might have been amused by the sight of Lord Stratford frustrated of a rich and suitable viscountess.

She did smile now as she recalled the look on Fliss and Darius's faces while they faced His Lordship on a sodden hillside track. Every look and gesture screamed they were lovers and Fliss did not look in the least bit sorry to turn her back on His Lordship's flattering offer. Then they all remembered Juno was still missing and never mind who would marry whom.

Lord Stratford was the girl's guardian and he had said they should all forget worrying about gossip. If the whole world knew she had gone missing, they just needed to find her—so now half the neighbourhood were out looking for the missing girl. Finding waiting for news at Miss Donne's more wearing than actively looking for Juno, Marianne was glad when Darius asked her to come back to Owlet Manor with his orders for the men today so he could stay in Broadley.

All these hours on, Marianne shook her head at her vivid mental image of Lord Stratford when she should be worrying about the still-missing Juno. In her shoes Marianne knew she would have bolted as well, however worrying it was not to have found the girl so many hours after she set out to walk the last stage of her long journey. Indeed, she *had* run away to marry Daniel, but that was a glorious adventure with him at the end of it. Marianne felt the bleakness of Daniel's death at the bloody siege of Badajoz more than two years ago threaten and there was always this hollow in her heart now. No Daniel to tease and quarrel and laugh with or to love with every breath in her body. How fiercely he would argue with her about that empty heart if he could hear her! He would insist she must live life to the full and love again, even if the best part of her was cut away the night he died.

Marianne shook her head at the bereft and gloomy place her tired mind had taken her when she was not paying attention. Things were better now. She was free of the suffocating respectability of genteel Bath society and her parents' compact new home. Darius inheriting Owlet Manor had rescued her from her mother and the condemnation of the Bath tabbies. She would rather scrub floors than go back there, so it was best to live in the moment and worry about the future when it got here.

And now the tall and fancifully twisted brick chimneys of Owlet Manor were visible above the sheltering trees at last and she was nearly home. A slender, dark-haired girl stepped out from behind the largest tree of all next to the grand gates of Owlet Manor nobody had shut for at least half a century. Marianne drew rein sharply and made Robin snort and shake his head in protest as she stared down at the girl and paid no attention to her horse this once. If she had not seen Lord Stratford first she might wonder if there was more than one girl wandering the countryside today, since this one was in quite the wrong place, but if there was a Defford stamp this girl had it. She was as dark haired as the viscount and her eyes the same clear bright blue.

Juno shot Marianne a wary look, her white teeth worrying at her lower lip like a child who knew she had not learned her lesson well enough. Marianne recalled Fliss worrying about the girl's painful shyness with strangers and bit back the rebuke for all the trouble she had caused that was trembling on her lips. The girl would bolt into the woods if Marianne was not careful and she had proved very good at being invisible when she chose, so goodness knew when they would manage to find her again.

'Good afternoon, Miss Defford,' she managed to say calmly. 'Would you like a seat in the gig for the last bit of the way to my brother's house?'

Juno shook her head, shot a frightened look towards the bustle and noise of the farmyards where the men must be thatching ricks and seemed to be on the edge of doing that bolt

Marianne was so worried about. The men were doing whatever it was with so much shouting and laughter Marianne guessed they had taken advantage of Darius's absence to drink a lot more cider than they should have this morning. She hoped the hay was dry under the tarpaulins before they began again or the wet grass could overheat and catch fire and that was the last thing Darius needed.

'Will you promise me not to run away again while I have Robin stabled and rubbed down? Miss Grantham has chewed her nails to the quick worrying about you and you must love her if you have come all this way to see her. I hope you will not let her suffer such painful anxiety for much longer by running away yet again.'

Juno looked shamefaced and shook her head, but that was not enough for Marianne. 'Promise me out loud that you will not bolt as soon as my back is turned,' she insisted with a stern look to say she would know if the girl lied.

'I promise,' she whispered and even managed to look Marianne in the eye so she supposed she would have to trust her.

'Very well, then. If you do not wish to be seen, follow the path over there. It winds around the house by the side of the lake and nobody in the stable yard or on the other side of the farm will be able to see you. There is a garden door round there and a bench where you can wait while I see to Robin and get the men working as they should be. I will have to get them to see the error of their ways while I am about it, so do not be surprised if it takes longer than either of us want it to.'

Juno surprised her with a shy smile and another shake of the head at the notion of Marianne ordering the farm workers about and them doing as she said.

'Having dealt with soldiers of most ranks and temperaments when I was with the army, those rogues are child's play,' she told the girl with a nod towards the noisy rickyard before she smiled back with mischief in her eyes. 'It is just a matter of learning how to handle them,' she added.

Juno shook her head again and looked dubious about the notion of even trying to understand what made most men tick.

'I will try not to be long,' Marianne prom-

ised with one last look at the diffident but determined girl who was already slipping into
the unkempt gardens like a wraith. Marianne
shook the reins to persuade patient Robin to
move on and tried not to look back as she
fervently hoped Juno Defford was a girl of
her word.

After handing out brusque orders to the
farm servants and a crushing rebuke to
make them see the error of their ways, Marianne made sure Robin was spoiled after his
gruelling day yesterday. She let herself into
the manor house by the back door as if in
no particular hurry lest any of the men were
watching her go, but as soon as it was shut
behind her she dashed across the hall to let
the girl in. Juno rose from the sun-warmed
bench and Marianne gave a sigh of relief.

'What the deuce are you doing here, young
lady?' she asked with all the effort and worry
of the last day making her sound brusque and
irritated.

'Miss Grantham told me about you and
your brother and this poor old house in her
letters,' Juno replied with a half-defiant, half-
apologetic look that said there might be more

of her uncle's fire in her than appearances suggested.

'Walking on past Broadley for the sake of curiosity would be cruel, so I hope you have a better reason for doing it. Miss Grantham is beside herself with worry.'

'I should never have sent that message. Nobody would have known I was here if I had not scribbled it in panic after I was robbed,' the girl said sulkily.

'And that would make everything all right, would it? You sound very young and foolish when you spout such rubbish and you put us through hours of worry today for no good reason. Can you even imagine what horrors Miss Grantham is dreading as the hours tick by with no sign of you?'

'I—' The girl broke off whatever she was going to say and Marianne saw her throat work as if she was fighting a sob. 'I will not go back to London and I will *not* marry that man. I would rather die.'

'Stop being such a tragedienne. Of course you must not marry a man who is so much older than you, especially if you do not even like him.'

Juno shook her head as if she could hardly believe someone was agreeing with her. She burst into overwrought tears as the strain and hardship of the last days and weeks caught up with her and Marianne drew the sobbing girl into her arms.

'I am a crotchety old woman to rip up at you like that when you have been having such a dreadful time, but we have been so worried about you,' she said to the top of the girl's head. 'And now I have made you cry when there are so many things we could be busy doing.'

'I am so sorry,' the girl managed to gasp out between sobs.

Marianne urged her back towards the ancient oak bench. 'Here, sit down and cry it all out,' she said and had to guide Juno's steps as she could not see for tears. Trying to will comfort into the weary and woebegone girl, Marianne recalled her little sister crying as bitterly seven years ago when Marianne had told Viola she was leaving home to find Daniel. If anything could have kept Marianne away from him, it would have been her sister's tears, but she had loved him too much to be swayed even by Viola's heartbreak. So she had gone anyway and the close bond between her and Viola had broken that night and the gap had never truly healed.

Her little sister had not written back when Marianne sent letters to tell her about her adventures as an army wife and tried to bridge the gulf between peaceful England and the war-torn lands where she had spent most of her married life. When she had come back, she was too full of pain and grief to reach out to her aloof and preoccupied teacher sister.

Then Viola had taken her current post as governess to Sir Harry Marbeck's wards and moved fifty miles from Bath and their parents' cramped house and it was too late. A few stiff letters since had not mended things and Marianne did not feel far from tears herself now. She smoothed Juno's tangled dark hair. 'Better?' she asked at a pause between sobs.

'Yes,' Juno said with a sigh that sounded as if it came from her boots and a hiccuping sob. 'Have you a handkerchief? I lost mine.'

Marianne dug in her unfashionable but convenient pocket and Juno wiped her eyes, then blew her nose a few times and held out the handkerchief. Marianne shook her head and was pleased when Juno managed a small chuckle. 'Not very appealing, is it?' she said.

'It can be washed. Speaking of washing— after you have done so, brushed your hair and eaten something, I expect you will feel much more ready to face the world again.'

'I am not sure I want to.'

'No? Well, I will have to send word to Miss Grantham you are safe and well and here with me so that she can call off the search and stop worrying about you.'

'Does Uncle Alaric have to know?'

'Alaric?' Marianne frowned and searched her memory for one of those. Oh, of course, the girl must mean Lord Stratford. 'Is that His Lordship's name?' Juno nodded. 'It suits him,' Marianne said unwarily.

'The first one was King of the Visigoths who sacked Rome. Uncle Alaric is not a barbarian.'

He had certainly looked like one when he had been filthy from the road, unshaven and tired half to death, her inner Marianne argued silently, and that reminded respectable

Mrs Turner how much trouble she had had with her inner siren this morning. Her silly fantasy of a pirate lover had been ridiculous, especially when he had turned out to be a viscount and way above her touch. 'Then why did you walk past Broadley and not let His Lordship and Miss Grantham know you are safe and well?'

'Because he might make me go back and I truly cannot live with Grandmama ever again after some of the things she said and did while we were in London, Mrs Turner. She told me she would lock me in my room until I agreed to marry Lord...' Juno paused as if she could not even bring herself to say the man's name. 'Anyway, I ran away before she could actually do it, but then I got to Worcester and...' Juno's voice tailed off as she remembered the disaster of being robbed and Marianne expected more distraught tears.

'I suppose you were right to run away—' she began to say.

'I *knew* you would understand,' Juno interrupted impulsively and gave a gusty sigh of relief.

'If there was no other way to make your

feelings plain to your suitor and your family, but it was very wrong of you to leave Miss Grantham and your uncle frantically searching for you today when you are quite safe. His Lordship must have ridden after you as if the devil himself was on his heels and I doubt from the look of him that the poor man has had much sleep since he left France.'

'I saw him. I hid behind a hedge when I heard a horseman coming and nearly stepped out when I saw it was Uncle Alaric, but he looked so grim and stern I did not dare. Maybe he is furious with me and has come to fetch me back and make me marry that horrid man and Grandmama was right all along and he did approve of the match. So that is why I came here to beg you to hide me, then get word to Miss Grantham, but ask her not to tell my family where I am because I would rather die than wed that—that man...' Juno paused as if she did not have words in her to describe how much she hated the lord her grandmother had been so determined to make her wed.

Marianne wondered what they had done between them to make Juno so revolted by the very idea of him she could not even say his name. From the almost childlike appeal in the girl's blue eyes she really hoped it had not been the ultimate in forced persuasion to make her agree she would have to marry a man who had ravished her. Heaven forbid, Marianne decided with a shudder. Sooner or later Fliss or Lord Stratford or maybe even Mrs Marianne Turner would have to try and persuade Juno to talk about what had happened to make the terrible risks of running away from all she knew to get here and escape that terrible situation seem worthwhile.

'I promise I will make myself useful and I would much sooner scrub floors and clean windows for the rest of my life than marry that awful old man. I know you work very hard because Miss Grantham said so in her letters and I am sure you could do with some help,' Juno said earnestly and that proved she was still more child than woman, did it not? To think she would just stay here and pretend the frantic search for her would die away and leave her in peace with Lord Stratford ransacking half the Welsh Marches for her was a world away from reality.

'Hiring yourself out as a housemaid until you are of age could never work. Lord Stratford nearly collapsed from shock and exhaustion when he found out you had not got to Broadley ahead of him, so we simply have to tell him you are safe, Juno. It would be cruel not to and you do not seem a heartless person to me.'

'No, I am not,' Juno said, her extreme youth obvious in her pout and refusal to meet Marianne's eyes and admit she was wrong to panic and come here instead of simply walking on into the town and saving herself and everyone else the extra trouble and effort of coming all the way out here. 'I suppose you are right,' she said at last.

'Can I trust you not to run away again while I write to tell Miss Grantham you are here and ask her to pass the news on to your uncle?'

'I did promise I would not,' Juno said and sounded so sulky and misused that Marianne nearly laughed. She resisted the urge as the girl was obviously in a fragile state and might take offence and flounce off if she did, promise or no.

'Good, then I will write a hasty letter and get our stable lad to deliver it before I come and find you again. Thank goodness the lad had enough sense to stay sober so he is in a fit state to ride Robin's brother Swift to Broadley.'

'I must hope he is not, then,' Juno said. 'Swift,' she explained when Marianne raised her eyebrows.

Chapter Four

Alaric knew it was a mistake to come, but he could not stay away. Even after the bath and shave Miss Donne had insisted on before he set out and the change of clothes he had needed for so long, he was not fit to do much more than sleep. But he had to see Juno with his own eyes and reassure himself she was safe, however foolish it was not to rest first and let her do so as well. At least every time his vision blurred and his brain threatened to shut down, his abiding sense of shame jerked him back to life again and urged him relentlessly on.

This was all his fault; he should have stayed in England and never mind his mother's open dislike of her only surviving child. It had been his duty to be sure Juno felt supported and loved during her first Season in town, even if he was too shallow to actually admit he loved his niece despite what her grandmother thought of both of them. What a fool he had been to think it would be better if he was not there to irritate the Dowager Lady Stratford and make Juno's debut a disaster. He shook his head to try to dismiss the fact his mother had hated him from the day he was born from his weary thoughts. He had always borne that burden and piling it on top of the guilt might make him forget the here and now and fall off this hard-mouthed and restive animal. He frowned at the road ahead because surely this back-of-beyond house of Yelverton's should be in sight by now? His latest hired horse was not an easy ride, but was every bit as fast as the ostler promised he would be.

Ah, there it was and a far more impressive house than expected, given Yelverton's rough manners and ruffian-like appearance this morning. As if he had any room to talk about appearances, Alaric chided himself and frowned at the streak of pale blue sky fighting the pall of cloud. Yelverton's home was nestled at the heart of a verdant valley and

soon Alaric would have no more time to rail
at himself for being a useless guardian. 'Aye,
and do not forget you are a loser in love as
well, Stratford, and Yelverton is the one you
lost to,' he reminded himself out loud, thinking it was high time he slept if he was talking to himself like a lunatic. 'Even if it was
not love between you and Miss Grantham,
she was your best chance of finding yourself a polite, well-bred and kind-hearted viscountess,' he added under his breath. It did
not help him feel any better now he had to
revise Yelverton's status up a notch from the
look of the substantial manor house up ahead.
The road twisted and turned yet again. Was
nothing in this confounded county straight
or direct? Ah, there it was again and Owlet
Manor was a fine and ancient gentleman's
residence. Alaric already owed the man respect for the fine military career Miss Donne
had outlined while Alaric ate a hot meal at
her insistence before he got back in the saddle to find this place.

The worst of his fears had faded when they
got that hasty message of Mrs Turner's to say
Juno was safe, but the flood of emotion he

felt on learning he could stop worrying about her safety had left him weak with relief. And this was no time for weakness when his niece clearly needed him to be strong. Despite his exhaustion he decided he simply had to see Juno with his own eyes and let her know he was sorry he had been such a poor guardian and protector, before he found a bed and slept for a week then thought a bit harder about his many sins of omission.

He blinked his eyes open wide again and realised he had almost nodded off in the saddle. He made himself take note of the land around the fine manor house growing ever larger on the horizon to keep himself awake. Closer in, he could see that the old house had been neglected for many a long year. The landlord in him could see that hard work and a little money had been spent on it lately. As the owner of prosperous estates he could offer Yelverton help getting this house and his land in order, if he happened to like him. As it was he had no intention of staying longer than it took him to remove Juno from Mrs Turner's care and get her back to Broadley, even if he had to beg the naggy-tempered and annoyingly unforgettable woman for the loan of her gig and a fresh horse to draw it with.

Tomorrow he would feel alive and awake enough to hire a carriage for the journey back to Stratford Park and a new life. He could worry about the details when they got there, but at least both of them would be excused his mother's cold dislike for the first time in their lives.

How could he have trusted the Dowager to put Juno's interests before her own? He had thought the obsessive love the woman had had for her eldest son would have rubbed off on George's only child, but apparently he was wrong about that as well as everything else. The Dowager Lady Stratford had told him she would never forgive Juno for being born female when they had had their last confrontation in London, before they finally washed their hands of one another and he galloped away. George's girl or not, Juno was a female, so she failed to keep the Dowager Lady Stratford's despised second son from inheriting his title and the fine estates that went with it. Of course she despised the silly chit, she told Alaric as if he was stupid not to have known it all along. And how could he have trusted Juno to his mother's care believing she must care because George was the girl's father?

'It suited you to believe in a fantasy, my lord,' he condemned himself disgustedly now.

Deep down he must have known his mother only had one chip of love in her stony heart and she had buried it with his brother. Alaric had given up trying to convince his mother he never wanted his brother's inheritance long ago, but he must have carried on dreaming impossible dreams when he passed Juno into her care after George's funeral and thought he had done the right thing. At seventeen he felt overwhelmed by the burdens that fell on him and poor little Juno was one more. But this was not about him and his excuses for behaving badly; it was about putting things right for Juno if he still could. He deserved to be so tired every bone in his body ached. He should feel the loss of an ideal wife in Miss Grantham. He had been a fool to leave her free to find and love a better man than careless, self-absorbed Alaric Defford. He truly hated himself as he dug his heels into his horse's flanks and urged the sullen animal on as fast as he would go.

He shot a disapproving look at rusted, open main gates to the venerable manor house's front door and rode on past. Grass was growing across the once-gravelled drive and there were so many weeds between the stone flags nearer the house that the flags were barely visible. He shook his head at such wanton neglect. He hoped Yelverton was ashamed of himself for not getting the path to his front door cleared straight away. How was the man's sister to receive polite visitors if they had to come in through the farmyard? 'Place is a shambles,' he muttered as he rode into the stable yard.

'Sir?' a slightly unsteady-looking farmhand asked warily, as if he thought he should have heard an order if his ears were up to it.

'Are you castaway?' Alaric demanded as he dismounted and staggered until the earth settled under his feet.

'If I am, that's two of us,' the man muttered, then stared back at Alaric with pretend innocence.

'Does your master know you despise his

kind?' Alaric asked with a steady look to let the rogue know he was not deceived by forelock tugging.

'He's bin a soldier, though, ain't he?' the man said as if that excused Yelverton's sins as one of the ruling elite.

Alaric decided he had heard quite enough about Saint Darius and his heroic past for today. 'Respect for his army service does not seem to have stopped you drinking in the middle of the day when you were supposed to be hard at work for him, though, does it?' he replied to let the fellow know he was not fooled by his act and taking advantage during a crisis was reprehensible.

'No, sir, but Mrs Turner ripped up at us so there's no need to join in. Said she was going to open the taps on the cider barrels until they was empty if we didn't get back to work, so she did,' the man said with a hint of male appreciation for a fine and spirited woman in his bleary eyes Alaric did not like one bit.

'Serve you all right if she did it anyway,' Alaric informed the man coolly. 'And kindly see that my horse is tended while I speak to the lady.'

The man gave a mocking salute that hit his ear instead of his forehead and Alaric decided Mrs Turner's wrath must have been mighty indeed to work its way past all that alcohol. He supposed he should be grateful she had managed to put the fear of God into her brother's workmen, since this one took the horse's bridle and led it towards the stables without another word. At least the nag would be inside and might get watered and maybe even fed to put it in a better temper for the return journey.

Alaric stopped frowning after the rebellious farmhand and frowned at the back of Owlet Manor instead. At least the narrow garden separating the house from the farmyards and the road was neat and newly planted with herbs and even one or two cottage-garden flowers to brighten it up. There was an old orchard to the side of the place that looked as if it had received some attention as well and a row of raspberry canes still glowed with the occasional red fruit the birds had not gobbled up. Mrs Turner's concerns were obviously more about food than decoration. Understandable if her brother did not have funds for more than the basics despite his grand house. Miss Donne had told him the manor and estate had fallen into the man's lap when he came home from the war.

Alaric eyed the narrow and mellowed Tudor brick on this side of the house and wondered how he would have felt if his grand heritage came with no money attached and years of neglect to make up for. Lucky that most Deffords had been careful landlords, then, and they never spent more than they could afford. It was no credit to him that he was a rich man and a lord, he decided as he noted the bricks needed pointing and the ancient oak porch was listing to one side like the farmhand who had done his best not to welcome Alaric to his master's new home. Ah well, none of it was any of his business, he decided and stepped through the porch to rap on the door.

'Yes, whatever is it this time?' Mrs Turner opened the door and demanded impatiently before she took the trouble to see who was out here.

Alaric supposed she had an excuse with all those fools half-drunk and maybe a little bit dangerous and her brother occupied else-where. 'Good afternoon,' he said with a silly echo of the awe and wonder that shot through him the first time he laid eyes on her trou-bling him again. He had hoped she would be less lovely and desirable than he recalled, but if anything he had undershot the mark.

'Oh, it is you,' she said as if he was the last person she wanted to see on her brother's doorstep even with a pack of half-cut rogues to be impatient with. 'I am sorry. Good day to you, Lord Stratford,' she said, sounding a lot more polite, but still not enthusiastic about their second doorstep of the day.

'I have come to see my niece,' he told her. She stood in the doorway as if trying to hide even the kitchen from his view and he was tempted to lift her aside and march in again, but could not bring himself to be so rude twice in a day.

'She is very tired,' she said and would not meet his eyes.

'I dare say, but I need to see for myself Juno is safe and well,' he insisted.

'You do not trust my word, Lord Stratford?'

'I do not know you, ma'am, and you seem

to be determined to prevent me seeing my ward.'

'It is not that,' she said uneasily.

'What *is* it, then?' he barked, nearly at the end of his tether. He would invade her brother's house to make sure Juno was whole and safe if he had to.

'I am sorry, my lord,' she said as if she really meant it, 'but Miss Defford does not wish to see you.'

He put out a shaking hand to steady himself against the door jamb and wished he could lean on this noble old house, let exhaustion wash over him so he could sleep standing up and forget about those hurtful words. If he slept long enough, maybe this nightmare would end and he would wake to a world of sanity and order. 'What do you expect me to do, then?' he asked lamely at last.

'Go back to Broadley and wait until you have both had a proper night's sleep and are feeling less exhausted and more rational,' Mrs Turner said as if she thought he could meekly ride back to that wretched little town without seeing for himself Juno was safe at last.

'I cannot leave here without knowing she is unharmed,' he allowed himself to plead.

Mrs Turner looked uneasy about keeping him standing out here like a beggar hoping for scraps. 'No, of course you cannot,' she murmured her agreement. 'Juno, you must show yourself and reassure your uncle you are safe and well,' she spoke up to his lurking niece and Alaric supposed he must be glad Juno did not bolt for the nearest attic to hide in when she realised he was coming. 'We cannot let His Lordship think we are holding you to ransom or whatever nonsensical ideas he will think up if you refuse to come out. No need to say a word if you would rather not, but you must prove to him you are well and in one piece, even if you are footsore and rather oddly dressed.'

He thought he heard a soft whisper of a laugh in the cool shadows beyond the kitchen and gazed hungrily past Mrs Turner's slender form, hoping for a glimpse of his niece. 'Just let me see you are unharmed, Jojo, and I promise you I will go away again until you are feeling better,' he said quietly and willed her to step forward. He loved his niece far more than he had ever been able to let her know, but he was the adult and he should have told her all through her lonely childhood if he wanted her to believe him now.

'You used to call me that when Papa was alive,' she said so softly he had to strain his ears for the words and he longed for her to come properly inside the room so he could catch a glimpse of her for the first time in far too long.

'And how he would rip up at me for letting his little girl be so miserable in London that you felt you had to come so far to find Miss Grantham.'

'You will not make me go back to live with Grandmama, will you?' she said and finally found the courage to peer around the door-post at him.

All he could see was two anxious blue eyes looking warily at him and her pale face looking thinner and even more worried than last time he had set eyes on her. Then he had been bidding her goodbye at his London home before he travelled on to Paris. 'No, even if I wanted to I could not since the Dowager has left the country and will live overseas from now on. I will not make you go anywhere you do not want to go ever again, Jojo,' he promised recklessly and with a wobble in his voice he wished Mrs Turner was not here to pick up on.

'I want to stay here,' Juno managed to say almost out loud.

Alaric's heart sank as he realised it could be too late to put his relationship with his niece right. Maybe he had defended himself against loving anyone for so long it had become a habit. But how could he have refused it to a child who had lost her father so young she could barely remember him? It seemed feeble and self-pitying to admit he had felt so shaken and alone when he lost his brother that he had built a wall around himself. Perhaps George had been lonely as his parents' only surviving child, but whatever the reason, he had taken to his baby brother and refused to hear their mother's orders to let the brat go to the devil and come away. Even as a boy he had taken care Alaric was happy and well looked after when he had inherited their father's title as a mere lad himself. George had always done his best to shield

Alaric from the Dowager's cold dislike and it had hit him like an Arctic blast when George was killed and Alaric had to step into his brother's shoes. Within the new Viscount Stratford's barricades he must have looked self-sufficient and composed instead of bereft and terrified. Men of power were certainly fooled and they began to use him for not quite official tasks like the one in Paris to help the Duke of Wellington through an awkward situation in any way he could. Little did they know there was a coward lurking behind all that lordly composure and now Juno had paid the price.

'Then so you shall, if I can make arrangements for your board and lodging and any other expenses. And if Mrs Turner does not mind having such a demanding young lady about the place when she has a great deal to do?'

I will miss you like the devil, but that will serve me right, he did not add. It would not be fair, after all he had not done for his niece up to now, to put any pressure on her to try and get her to love him back. Serve him right if he never did after walling her out along with the rest of the world ever since her father died.

'You really do not mind if I stay, then?' Juno said and she was so eager to hear his reply she actually crept past the doorway and stood just inside the room like a feral kitten ready to bolt for cover if he made the slightest move towards her. 'I promise not to get under your feet, Mrs Turner,' she added earnestly. 'I know you are very busy, but I would love to help you clean and sort through all the curious old things you have found. Miss Grantham made it sound such an adventure I feel as if I know you and the house already.'

'I wonder if she knows how hard that work can be. It is rough and ready living here, Juno. I have a great deal to do before this old place even feels like a proper gentleman's residence once again. If you really want to stay with us for a while and rough it and His Lordship is content for my brother and me to have you here until you have recovered from your long journey, then I am sure we would be very happy to have you stay here until you feel you are ready to face the world again.'

Mrs Turner was clearly waiting to hear

whether he was resigned to his niece's wishes, if not exactly delighted by them. He could see the knowledge that Miss Grantham would shortly be part of this household in her eyes as she met his with something like an apology because his niece seemed to prefer her company to his.

'His Lordship must be content if that is what you really want, Juno,' he said wearily. 'I hope you will write to me now and again,' he allowed himself to beg before he could make himself go away and leave her with strangers.

'Yes,' she said and seemed to hesitate, as if she wanted to say more, but was afraid he might try to change her mind if she risked it.

'Good,' he said hoarsely and fought back some unmanly feeling tears as he shook his head and managed to meet Mrs Turner's gaze with a plea in his. 'Look after her for me, please?' he asked and he did trust her to do that, stranger as she was and not a particularly polite or respectful one either.

'I will,' she promised.

'Very well, then. I wish you good day, Mrs Turner, Juno,' he said gruffly and bowed, then turned on his heel before he lowered himself to beg her to trust him instead. Time to get on with the rest of his life without most of the things he thought he had when he left England on that disastrous errand to France, where it turned out nobody wanted him very much either.

Chapter Five

A tense silence settled over the usually comfortable kitchen where Marianne often sat with Darius of an evening rather than make him change back into a gentleman after his labours on the farms all day. She listened to the noise of Lord Stratford's finely made boots on the cobbles fade from hearing and wondered what Juno was thinking as she decided they sounded very lonely. She doubted Lord Stratford would want her pity, but he had it for the slap his timid niece had just landed on him without lifting a finger.

'I could not go with him, Mrs Turner, really I could not.' There was a look very like guilt on the girl's face when Marianne turned to look at her surprise guest's face.

'Well, you are not doing so, are you?' she said coolly. In her opinion forgiving someone who sincerely rued a mistake was part of being grown up and Juno was using her youth and shyness as an excuse not to do so. She supposed she should not judge the girl harshly; Juno had obviously been through a few horrible months at the mercy of an unsympathetic grandmother and the indifferent *ton*. She smiled at the girl to take the sting out of her question and thanked her lucky stars she was not rich or noble enough to be looked down on and ignored by the cream of polite society herself.

'No, but thank you for agreeing to take me in.'

'It can only be for a while, Juno. You belong with your family and I think Lord Stratford will pay much more attention to your wants and needs from now on. You have put him through a dreadful ordeal by disappearing as if you had been stolen away by the fairies and I suspect he has learnt his lesson well and will take much better care of you in future.'

'Maybe, but I still do not want to be a useless lady who sews seat covers, paints dreadful watercolours and plays the harp badly until some lord is ready to marry me for the sake of my dowry and an heir.'

Juno sounded downright sulky now and looked like an overwrought child sadly in need of her bed. Marianne sighed and supposed the girl was not so very far from the schoolroom. She certainly did not seem anywhere near mature enough to face the scarily adult dilemma she had been forced into by her grandmother. Under her crippling shyness Marianne thought the girl was angry because her uncle had not been there when she needed him most. She was certainly being unfeeling about Lord Stratford's exhausting ride and obvious weariness when he got here, but maybe he deserved it. Marianne still felt guilty about sending him back to Broadley without his niece, though. At least Lord Stratford cared enough about the girl to ride so hard he looked almost asleep on his feet now the relief of finding out Juno was safe had removed the worst of his worries about her.

'We can put the knotty problem of your future aside for now and think about what comes next instead. I would be very glad of your help with my endless pile of mending and I promise to stitch any seat covers that are in need of repair so you do not have to do it.'

Juno grimaced at the thought of sitting quietly and sewing after all the drama of the last few days, but if she thought it would be a nice little holiday from real life to stay here she might as well find out straight away nobody was allowed to sit idly by when there was so much to do. It would do Juno no harm at all to perform a few boring tasks. Marianne planned to talk about even more boring things while they worked, since she doubted Juno would agree to go up to bed and sleep off the worst of her adventures in the middle of the day. If she was good enough at her tedious tales, she might even allow herself to nod off and catch up on some much-needed sleep.

Suddenly there was a cacophony of barking and outraged neighs through the open door, followed by an ominous thud, then the sound of men shouting and arguing at the tops of their voices. Alarm spurred her into action before her mind caught up and Marianne's heart thudded with dread as she ran outside with her skirts lifted high to free her legs for action. She hardly knew the man, but fear for Lord Stratford rang around her head in a near panic. Of course she would feel like this about any human being who could have been gravely injured in what sounded like a crashing fall. Juno was right behind her now and Marianne hoped she would not shy away from whatever trouble was ahead of them and faint or get in the way.

The yard was full of men shouting and milling about and the farm dogs were still barking and that dratted horse was stamping about, looking wild-eyed and dangerous. There was Lord Stratford in the midst of it all. He was lying too still with the horse dancing and snorting with its deadly iron-shod hooves far too close to the man's prone body as it looked wild enough to lash out with intent to kill.

'Joe Nicklin, you catch that damned horse right now, before it kills the poor man,' Marianne shouted over the hullabaloo at the most sober of the men who had gathered to gawp at the chaos and argue about the fallen man at the centre of it. Thankfully Joe listened to her and made a lunge at the animal's bridle, then wrestled the beast back and away so at least it was no longer within kicking reach of Lord Stratford's dark head. Seeing Joe spring into action, the rest of the men seemed to snap out of their panicked stupor and ran to help Joe force the foam-flecked and still-protesting horse away from its fallen rider. 'We will talk about who did what, when and why once I am quite certain His Lordship will survive,' she added with a quelling glare at anyone still standing about gawping.

'Right you are, missus,' Joe's brother Seth said with an ingratiating smile. He was trying too hard to placate her and her suspicion he had something to do with this disaster hardened to a certainty. Seth was a troubled soul who had come back from the war restless and edgy and inclined to lose his temper without much cause, but he was also a superb horseman. She suspected Darius had taken him on because he recognised the faraway look in the man's eyes when he spoke of war and her brother had a soft heart under his self-contained manner. But never mind them now, Lord Stratford needed all her attention until he was his arrogant self again and she refused to believe in an alternative.

'Ride for the doctor as fast as you can go and insist he comes back with you, Seth. Tell him it could be a matter of life and death and say who is injured and if you do it well enough maybe whatever mischief you have been about today need go no further,' she ordered brusquely and at least he had the shame or wit enough to run off to the stables and not stand about arguing.

'And you can get that bad-tempered brute out of the way, Joe,' she snapped as the nag still fought the man's powerful grip. 'Put him in a stall and make it as dark as you can get it, then leave him to do his worst. We can worry about him later.'

Now Marianne's eyes were fixed on Lord Stratford's prone body as she tried to see if any of his limbs were bent under him at a worrying angle. Somehow the sight of him so vulnerable and undefended made her blink back a tear. She ordered herself not to be such a widgeon and get on with finding out what was wrong with him and whether it could be put right. Her heart was in her mouth as she walked past the men dragging the still-resisting horse away to kneel at his side.

Juno sank onto her knees at her uncle's side even before Marianne got there. 'Do not even think about moving him. We must find out how bad his injuries are before we risk making bad worse,' Marianne ordered when the girl reached out to touch him, then snatched her hand back as if it had been bitten at the thought of doing him more harm.

'Is he going to die, Mrs Turner? It will be my fault if he does. He would not even be here to be thrown from that brute if not for me.'

'Pray do not start spouting such morbid nonsense when I need your help. You are the only truly sober person here so do not have hysterics.'

'What must I do, then?'

'Stay calm while I find out how badly he is injured,' Marianne said, and began to explore Lord Stratford's prone body as gently as she could as she fought back her own panic and this silly feeling that if he was mortally injured it would feel like a personal tragedy. She hardly even knew him. Thank goodness she had a good deal of experience nursing wounded men who stood a better chance of recovery if they could stay with the column than they would in an army hospital.

She decided none of his limbs looked twisted out of shape and began gently winnowing through his crisply curling dark hair until she found a knotty lump underneath it already beginning to swell and explaining his loss of consciousness. 'He will certainly have a headache when he wakes up,' she told Juno with as much of a smile as she could manage to reassure the girl.

'He will hate that,' Juno said with a wobble in her voice to say she knew how serious head injuries could be, but if hoping for the best would help she was ready to try it. 'Uncle Alaric hates being ill.'

'Then he is in for a torrid time. I think he has sprained his wrist as well. Was the gentleman slammed against the wall, Joe?' Marianne asked the man as he ran back into the yard. At least he must have shut the bad-tempered nag away and the men looked as if this accident had sobered them up so they might be in a fit state to help her get His

Lordship inside without further endangering his life.

'Seth brought his horse out. I was thatching the rick like you said I was to, Mrs Turner. I only looked over here when our Seth shouted the horse was getting ready to bolt and it must have thrown yon lord against the wall before Seth could grab it and make it stop. Bad-tempered great brute it is. I wonder the Royal George hired him out to a proper lord.'

'I expect he was in a hurry and demanded the fastest horse they had in their stables,' Marianne said and fought the oddest feeling she knew him that well while she ran exploring hands over surprisingly heavy bands of muscle on His Lordship's torso as gently as she could to find out if he had any more serious injuries they needed to worry about.

'He would do that. He does not like to wait,' Juno agreed almost fondly.

Marianne carried on with her exploration. Now she knew Lord Stratford did not have a spare ounce anywhere on his impressively muscular body and she should not be impressed by the strength and endurance of the man at a time like this. She soothed the gentlest of touches over his waist and narrow hips and even lying in a heap like this she could tell his legs were the same length. At least there was no need to worry about a serious fracture that could put his life in danger from internal bleeding. His left ankle seemed awkward, though, and she dreaded having to cut the snug-fitting riding boot off it so she could see if it was broken. Best do it before he was awake and would feel every agonising movement and she might flinch with him and risk cutting him instead. 'I need the boning shears from the scullery, Juno. Take care, they are very sharp and please do not run on the way back—I do not have time for any more patients,' she said and Juno was gone before she even finished her sentence.

Lord Stratford was lying worryingly still, but breathing evenly. He would wake up to a dreadful headache, a sore wrist and maybe a broken ankle, so perhaps it was as well if he stayed unconscious a little longer. She spared a moment to admire the stern symmetry of his features as he lay undefended. Without his challenging blue gaze to argue he was aloof and self-contained, she could see how sensitive his mouth was when he did not have it under strict control. Now the lines of exhaustion around it were relaxed he also looked as if he was born to laugh a lot more than he did.

Being lord of so much must lie heavy on his broad shoulders and the real Alaric Defford was far more fascinating than Lord Stratford, with his lordly orders and air of owning half the world and having designs on the rest. Was it all a front, then? Having heard him with Juno before this disaster she suspected it might well be and tried hard not to pity him for needing to keep one up even with his nearest and dearest.

'Well done,' she said when Juno reappeared with the sharpest scissors they had in the house, then slipped back into her place at her uncle's side. 'Be careful,' Marianne warned her as she gripped the shears herself and gritted her teeth ready for action. 'He might grip down on your hand hard if this wakes him up. He is sure to be in a great deal of pain one way and another and he will not be in a fit state to consider who or what he has hold of.'

'Worry about him, I can look after myself.'

'So you can,' Marianne said as she slipped the cold metal under his once beautiful boot and made herself cut through the supple leather.

Alaric was having a wonderful dream where he drifted between sleep and happy fulfilment in Mrs Turner's bed. Her sky blue eyes were soft and heavy lidded with sleep and sensual satisfaction his dream self felt smug about. Warmth and openness and a heady passion weighed their limbs down in this soft bed with its fine linen sheets. He could smell the summer breezes and lavender on them as well as sated desire and breathed in the fresh scent and pure essence of Mrs Turner. He wondered why he did not know her first name as they were so gloriously intimate. Mary? What had Miss Donne called her when they first met? Margaret? No, Marianne. He recalled her name with satisfaction; first, because he liked it and, second, because it suited her. And it was always as well to remember a lady's name when you bedded her to their mutual and lingering pleasure.

A good romantic name it was, too, just right

for a fine woman with lovely eyes and the slender, long-limbed body he had lusted after so fiercely at first glance. There, at least he had the trick of her name now, so he would not have to call her by another man's surname when they woke up in the morning for an even more blissful loving by daylight after this night of it he could not remember even beginning with her. He was very willing to go on now they were here and very much together in the private summer night, but that lack of memory troubled him even in his dreams.

Now he came to think of it, there was a deal of noise around in what should be a peaceful and private bedchamber in the middle of the night as well. And it felt as if the sun was beating on his head, which was wrong for the night-time, and there was a breath of wind against his cheek as well which did not seem to match a slumberous bedchamber in the blessed darkness. And this mattress was devilish uncomfortable all of a sudden. His dream began to spiral away and he could feel a stone under his hip. Even in the worst inn he had ever come across he doubted they had any of those in their mattresses.

The last shards of his lovely fantasy began to shatter as pain ran in to take its place with an evil chuckle. He frowned against the loss of what felt like earthly paradise and screwed up his eyes to protest at the light. He wished whoever was making that confounded row would be quiet so he could go back to sleep.

'He is waking up at last,' Juno said. What was she doing here? He hoped his innocent niece had not seen him slip out of Mrs Turner's bed to deal with the idiot groaning in what sounded like agony when they were all trying to sleep.

'Can you remember your name?' Mrs Turner's otherwise pleasant contralto voice demanded.

What a question to ask a man who had to deal with the idiot while he had agony coursing through him like hot knives. She grasped his good hand and squeezed it as if ordering him not to ignore her. 'Your name?' she nagged and he was far too busy with the idiot to reply to such a silly question, but he supposed he ought to oblige a lady.

'I am Alaric Defford. I wish someone would tell that fool to be quiet and let me sleep,' he murmured.

'What fool?' Marianne Turner asked as if wondering about his sanity.

'The one who keeps moaning and groaning like an idiot.'

'That is you, Uncle Alaric,' Juno said and he felt his way up through another layer of unconsciousness and immediately wished he had stayed down there.

'Is it? Then I must have been swearing as well,' he admitted and opened his eyes to look up at his niece and hope she had not been listening. Agony bit as the sunlight bored into his flinching eyeballs and made him swear all over again as a jag of pain joined up with the one at the back of his aching head and ripped through him like hot iron.

'So sorry, Jojo,' he murmured and felt her hand tighten on his. Somehow he must find a way to cut himself off from the pain and protect her from it. 'Bad uncle,' he managed to say lamely before he shut his eyes again. He wished someone would turn off the sun so the inside of his eyelids were not such a fiery red. Shade might reduce the agony to a bearable hum and maybe he could gather his senses enough to open his eyes again and find out exactly what was going on.

'No, you are the best of uncles,' Juno argued with a tremble in her voice.

Somehow he managed to force his eyelids open again and never mind the thunderclap he knew was waiting for him this time. He had to let her know he was back in the land of the living and intending to stay here.

'Lie still and be quiet,' Marianne Turner ordered him softly and he was glad to do as he was bid for once.

She had put herself between him and the sun as well. He was almost ready to worship her thoughtfulness, although he wished his dream of her as his willing and about-to-be-sated-again lover was the reality he had woken up to instead of this one. In this world Mrs Marianne Turner had disliked him on sight and did not warm to him much afterwards. She was not likely to be impressed when he moaned and groaned and swore in his sleep, so there was very little chance of that rich fantasy ever coming true.

'Gladly,' he muttered and wondered when the sledgehammer inside his head would stop beating. Then he realised he could half hear and half feel a new sort of thunder through the very ground he lay on. He seemed to be in danger of being trampled by a herd of runaway horses or panicked cattle. He vaguely remembered the ill-tempered nag he rode in on taking offence at something before dreams and that very seductive fantasy took over his head and blotted out the pain and shock of being thrown. Maybe he should get up and run, but it felt beyond him so he lay as still as he could and waited for the next calamity to strike him. 'Run!' he muttered urgently to Juno and Marianne and tried to force his eyes open and even felt for strength to put himself between them and whatever was about to run them down.

'Oh, Darius, I am so very glad to see you,' he heard Marianne Turner call out with apparent delight as the noise of what he could now tell was a single horse's racing hooves halted sharply. Alaric finally managed to open his eyes just in time to see Darius the

Paragon leap off it and run towards them like a stunt rider.

'Wonderful,' Alaric said with all the irony he had available at short notice.

'Good Gad, Nan, what has the noble idiot done to himself this time?' Yelverton exclaimed as if Alaric had fallen off his horse on purpose.

He actually felt sick with dislike because it was better than being sick with pain. He did not want to humiliate himself in front of his niece and the lovely Mrs Turner. Loathing Darius Yelverton for being whole and hearty and not in pain, as well as in love with the woman Alaric thought he wanted to marry until he came here, would have to do instead. Although his yearning for Marianne Turner in his bed even when he was knocked out whispered he had not wanted to marry Miss Grantham anywhere near as passionately as she deserved her husband to want to marry her.

'I am not sure it was his fault this time,' Marianne said.

Alaric dared open one eye against the afternoon sun to look up at her. She seemed to be staring at a hangdog-looking man just within his field of vision and he did not have the slightest inclination to get a better look at the unshaven lout so he peered up at her instead. He decided dreamily he had no great interest in anyone else with her to fix his gaze on instead and managed to forget how much his head ached for a lovely moment.

She had a sharply determined chin to add an edge to her oval face. It rescued her from mere prettiness and pushed her towards a fugitive sort of beauty. So much of her compelling attraction lay in her moods and expression that he had to wonder how she would go on in his exclusive circle of almost friends. No doubt Marianne would be fascinating and full of life and spirit if she chose to let her true nature out in public, but quiet and avoiding the limelight if she did not. What a conundrum of a woman she was and of course he had met lovelier women and even managed to bed one or two of them, but they would all fade to insignificance next to her.

That lovely mouth of hers was too generous for classical beauty and her nose a little too pert, but even in a room full of accredited beauties he would still find her compelling and the rest all but invisible. Her face had a unique charm that made her beauty lifelong instead of a fleetingly perfect thing made of youth and beauty and a generous hand from Mother Nature.

He also liked the fact her honey-gold curls were coming down again, despite all the pins she must have skewered into it to pin the heavy weight under that ugly cap. Why on earth did she keep trying to turn herself into a quiz when a man would have to be blind or daft not to see the intense blue of her intelligent gaze and the kissable softness of her lips? 'Impossible,' he murmured to argue with her cap and maybe his wits had gone begging after all.

'I will have an accounting for this later,' Yelverton was saying grimly to the silent men even Alaric could practically hear shuffling their feet and longing to get away from the man's best officer's glare.

Alaric did not have the slightest inclination to watch Yelverton instead of his sister and work out exactly what had happened. He lay here and was glad that Marianne had not transferred all her attention to her brother as she shook her head at him and shrugged to say she had no idea what he was talking about. 'Impossible what?' she asked him as everyone else was occupied with who had done what and why and it did not matter a jot as he lay still and admired the rich brown and gold and even the odd red light in her hair.

'Do you think we dare move him, Marianne?' Yelverton interrupted them and from the sound of his voice he was much closer now.

Alaric bit back a protest. He was likely to faint again if they even tried it and that would be the final humiliation, but he could hardly say so without sounding feeble.

'We must keep his head still and he is covered in bruises and has a swollen ankle to consider although luckily I do not think it is broken. We managed to cut his boot off before it swelled up too badly and I dare say a cold compress would make it feel a lot more comfortable once we can get him to bed and put one on it.'

'At last, something to look forward to,'

Alaric murmured and heard her chuckle very softly.

He felt stupidly elated to share even a moment of irony with her, but dreaded losing any dignity he had left if they tried to help him up and he lost consciousness again or cast up his accounts. He wished he could snap his fingers and be out of this bright sunlight for a while before he need set out for Broadley again, though. Juno's hand tightened on his good one as if his flinch at the idea of his hurts being disturbed pained her.

'Perhaps you would like to pass out while we get you inside, Stratford,' Darius Yelverton loomed over him to say half-seriously and Alaric longed for the strength to plant him a facer.

'I think I hate you,' he muttered when the man was close enough to peer into his eyes as if checking them for dust motes.

'I know you do right now,' the man joked and grinned at Alaric as if he understood him all too well.

Chapter Six

It galled him to oblige Yelverton, but Alaric woke up hours or maybe even days later in the feather bed he had been dreaming about earlier. Except this time it felt lonely in here and there was a wary sort of silence around him. He lay still and thought about the world and his place in it and concluded it felt like night-time. He must have been out of his senses for a long time, then. He was quite happy for it to have been days if that got him closer to the end of this weakness and the pain trundling through his battered body like a bullock cart now he was awake again. He shifted against the summer-scented sheets he was fantasising about earlier and bit back a groan.

Keep still, then, man, he reasoned impatiently and tried to track down the pain.

He needed to find out if it was safe to move any of his aching body without a humiliating scream. If he stayed still, he only ached all over, but he knew real pain was lying in wait like a grinning demon carrying a pitchfork to prod him with. He tried to shift his arm, but his wrist shot a burning pain through it whenever he tried to move so it seemed sensible not to. He had to fight an urge to fidget and see if one place in this bed was better than another. Maybe he could curl into a ball and find comfort somewhere. He felt bruised from head to toe and, talking of toes, one of his feet felt just as usual, but the other throbbed if he tried to move it. So that was a wrist and a foot out of action.

He frowned and felt that horrible pounding hammer start up in his head again. A savage blow to the head must be his most dangerous hurt, then. What if he had lost his wits? What would become of Stratford Park and all the farms and cottages? So many people depended on him for a roof over their heads and bread in their bellies but, worst of all, what about Juno? If he was addled, who was going to take care of his niece until she came of age?

His mother was her only other close relative and Alaric shuddered away from the very idea of leaving Juno completely at her lack of mercy ever again. Under the provisions of the will he had made a decade ago when he came of age, Juno would inherit all the unentailed land and his private fortune when he died. Every fortune hunter in the British Isles would try to marry her by fair means or foul. At least half would not mind if it was only held in trust because he was locked up in a madhouse as they could then borrow against her expectations. The poor girl would become an object to be bought and sold rather than a sensitive being with the right to make her own choices in life. So he simply had to be well and sane. That was the only way to make sure Juno was who she wanted to be.

He made himself open his eyes, then blinked against the pain as his vision cleared and he found himself staring up at Mrs Marianne Turner's unique set of feminine features yet again. This time her face was shadow softened and he wondered if he had conjured her from his dreams and blinked again. As she was still here, at least he had not imagined her the first time.

'Are you in a great deal of pain, my lord?' she whispered as she misread his frown.

'A little, but please will you tell me if my wits are addled before I worry about anything else, Marianne,' he pleaded urgently. Her given name slipped out, but keeping guard on his tongue did not seem important with the threat of madness hanging over him. 'I beg your pardon, Mrs Turner,' he corrected himself impatiently when she frowned at him as if he was talking another language.

'As far as I can tell on less than a day's acquaintance, you are sane as you ever were,' she told him with a shrug, as if she had her doubts about his sanity at their first meeting on Miss Donne's doorstep, so that was not very sane at all.

'Good,' he murmured. 'Is it still today, then?' he asked as the rest of her words sank in. It felt as if far more time should have gone by since he first set eyes on her, but at least he had not lost days or even weeks lying here like a block.

She took a workaday sort of man's watch case out of her pocket, flicked it open and held the timepiece up to the shaded candle flame he supposed had been masked for his benefit. He silently thanked her for that, knowing even a candle's worth of light shining into his eyes would hurt like hell.

'Two o'clock in the morning,' she told him briskly, 'so it is actually tomorrow if you wish to be strictly accurate.'

'Thank you, it seems as well. While we are being precise, you might as well tell me what other injuries I have sustained.'

'Are you sure you want to know?' she asked with the wry smile he was beginning to watch out for. Teaching himself not to do that was another task he could face when he was feeling better.

'If I am of sound mind and need to remake my will because my life is in danger, I need to know about that so it can be done properly this time and my niece will be protected from fortune hunters and her property being taken over by the Crown estate,' he told her very seriously. Juno's future was much too important for him to be careless about it any longer.

'According to Dr Long, you have been very lucky although I would argue. You have to stay in a dark room for several days so we can make sure you suffer no lasting damage from that blow on the head and it is hardly good luck to be thrown against a stone wall by a bucking horse. None of the hurts you sustained will be life threatening as long as you are patient and do not go galloping across the country on another mad ride for a month or so and stay in bed until all danger of worse consequences than a headache have passed.'

The thought of his headache jarring if he even got on a horse made another mad dash across country seem unthinkable. He was more frustrated by her constant 'my lording' than the idea of not being able to get out of bed. It felt as if they should be beyond distinctions of rank by now, but he supposed he was forced on her and her brother, so he would just have to endure her reminders of who he was and how poorly he fitted in here. 'What about those other injuries you mentioned, how bad are they?'

'You must know you have sprained your wrist by now since you tried to move it and flinched and you have sprained and perhaps broken your ankle.'

He must have looked horrified by the possibility of not being able to walk or ride properly for a month or so. She gave him a wry smile and a sympathetic shake of her head. Where were lordly aloofness and hard-won self-control now? Lost like a highwayman's mask, he decided, and only just stopped himself shaking his head because he knew it would hurt.

'I suppose the amount of time your ankle takes to heal will let us know whether it is broken or sprained. And as for your head and the amount of time you have spent sleeping since you knocked yourself out on that wall, the ridiculous ride you put yourself through to get here faster than a man was meant to travel accounts for most of that, if you ask me. Dr Long was worried the pain of being moved did not wake you, but he did not see you at dawn on Miss Donne's doorstep so he has no idea you were a fool to start with, my lord. At least two days' worth of hard riding and your refusal to be sensible even before you insisted on riding here because you did not trust me to look after Juno meant you have had less sleep than your body needs for several days. In my opinion Mother Nature simply took over, Lord Stratford, and your head injury is not as severe as the doctor fears. Your long sleep only proves your body has more sense than the rest of you.'

'He is a doctor,' Alaric said with only half his mind on what he was saying. The rest was worrying at the threat still hanging over him that the blow on his head was more serious than they hoped and how he wished she would stop calling him Lord Stratford all the time. He did not feel like a correct and aloof viscount, lying here like a helpless infant. He wished she really was Marianne to him and not just a stranger so she might call him Alaric and soothe and nag him out of affection instead of duty to an injured stranger.

'Of a sort,' Marianne said dismissively and where were they? Ah, yes, doctors—he had little interest in them at the best of times. 'I met one or two like him when I was with the army,' she went on as if she agreed with him for once. 'They believe in malign providence rather than a duty to heal the injured. In my experience cleanliness and patience mend more hurts than the sawbones' gloom and purges.'

'You were with the army?' Alaric asked incredulously.

'My husband was a soldier,' she said and he thought she must be very weary herself to let him see the sadness and faraway look in her eyes, as if she was with her absent Mr Turner in spirit even if she would not be seeing him again this side of the grave.

'I am sorry for your loss,' he said sincerely, presuming on that past tense.

'So am I,' she said very quietly, then seemed to make an effort of will to snap herself out of the lonely place memory of Lieutenant or Captain Turner, or however high her late husband rose, had taken her. 'And you need more sleep in order to heal. I forgot to add you are bruised black and blue all down the side of your body that hit my brother's newly mended wall to the list of your injuries, Lord Stratford,' she told him softly but sternly, as if he might not know he was aching like the devil.

'I must have had a deal of rest already. It was no more than an hour or two after midday when I let that bad-tempered nag throw me and you say it is the middle of the night now. You are the one who is in need of sleep now, Mrs Turner. I seem to have had plenty of it to be going on with.'

'Someone has to sit with you in order to make sure you do not get out of bed and ride off into the night. Juno is too young for this much responsibility and quite worn out after all the walking and worrying she did on the way here. My brother has to be up early tomorrow to take charge of the men after yesterday's shenanigans, so I persuaded him go to bed as well.'

'You should have a chaperone,' he argued and frowned when she chuckled as if the very idea was ridiculous. 'Of course you should—you are hardly at your last prayers and neither am I.'

'You are not in any state to endanger anyone and the widow of a common soldier is not bound by the same rules as a Miss Defford, my lord,' she said and her set mouth and steady gaze dared him to be shocked by the man she had married.

Yes, he was shocked and her family must have been disappointed by the match, but she still looked like a lady to him. It must have taken great courage to defy the conventions and marry her soldier anyway. 'So you feel free to make up your own rules?' he said and there was a flicker of doubt in her eyes as if he had put his finger on something she did not want the rest of the world to know.

'I am free *not* to paint watercolours or embroider fire screens or perform good works the poor probably do not want if that is what you mean. I fear I was never a properly genteel young lady, my lord, and at least I do not even have to pretend I want to be one any more.'

He wanted to laugh out loud, but did not dare, first, because it would jar his bruises and, second, because she would be offended. She would never be quietly, boringly compliant with society's sillier edicts about what a lady could and could not do if she lived to be a hundred. Did that make her less of a lady?

No, he matched her to the best examples of her kind and decided character and charm triumphed over the lack of it every time. 'Are you an improper one, then?' he joked carelessly and saw contempt in her eyes before she turned away as if looking for a better distraction than him in this pared-back bedchamber.

'I shall never marry again and no lover could compare to my late husband, so I shall not be taking one of those either, my lord, before you ask,' she said very firmly indeed and squared her chin as if he might argue and would be wasting his breath.

He recognised a false trail when he heard one and ignored that slur on his supposed nobility. So her brother had been trying to persuade her to consider a second marriage, had he? Yes, he must have done for her to be looking at him so sternly she clearly thought he was joining a male conspiracy against her. And did she really think he wanted to be one of those lovers she was so determined not to have? If so, she was right. He did not blame Yelverton for doing what any responsible brother would rather than see his sister

lonely or pestered by rakes and rogues for
the rest of her life. She was dangerously unaware of her own looks and, even if most of
him had no intention of offering her a carte
blanche, he could have provided a compre-
hensive list of her form and features blind-
folded and after barely as day's acquaintance.
No wonder her brother was worried.

She would be happier and safer with a husband to fight off the wolves if only she would
consider the idea. Of course, if she was wed,
she would not be here for him to gawp at like
an overheated youth. If she had an eager lover
waiting for her to come back to his bed, my
Lord Stratford would have woken up alone
and bewildered in a strange bed and that
would never do.

'What will you do when your brother mar-
ries Miss Grantham?' he asked, using up
all the tolerance an invalid could play on in
one go. But at least he could talk about Miss
Grantham's wedding to another man without
a trace of disappointment she was not marrying him. He was not jealous of Titian-haired,
quietly lovely, well-bred and accomplished
Miss Grantham and Squire Yelverton. Only

yesterday, he had thought he was bereft and humiliated when it became obvious those two lovers had spent the night together in every sense of the word. Now the very idea of a marriage of convenience with Juno's former governess seemed to belong to a different world, along with an Alaric Defford he did not know or understand any more. That blow on the head must have been more severe than she thought.

'For now I shall be busy getting this lovely old place back in good enough order to house their guests, then I suppose I will have to find another house in need of care and attention and apply for the post of housekeeper. My perfect employer would be a reclusive elderly lady so I did not have to avoid the gossips or be put to the trouble and mess of entertaining her non-existent friends.'

'I doubt the world will ever be incurious about you, Mrs Turner, even if it was ready to oblige your solitary and bad-tempered employer by staying away,' he warned half-seriously because the idea of her as anyone's housekeeper was absurd.

He hated the idea of her at anyone's beck

and call year after year, growing careworn and depressed as day followed day in a relentless procession of sameness and duty. He shuddered to think what her life would be like if she had to work for a man instead of an elderly lady as the dog was sure to try and take advantage. His fists tightened under the covers and pain shot through his damaged wrist.

'No, you are quite wrong,' she argued earnestly. 'I would work hard and I am not important enough for anyone to take notice of, my lord.'

'All this "my lording" is sheer flummery,' he surprised them both by saying wearily. 'And worldly rank and jostling for position in high society means nothing next to family and true friends.'

She was silent, as if carefully weighing up what to say to a viscount who did not want to be one any more and they both knew he had no choice about the matter. He felt guilty and a bit stupid for letting his confusion about his life out to someone he did not even know this time yesterday. Was this a concussion after all, then, or the after-effects of his long ride and all that terrifying anxiety for Juno as Marianne claimed? Maybe he felt low because he had wasted so much time behaving as a viscount should. He recalled his horror that Juno was hiding from *him* this afternoon with a shudder and a yawning gap threatened to open inside him and let loneliness flood in. Juno did not trust him; she thought he came after her to make her wed against her will and that hurt more than any bruise or sprain or sore head.

'It seems to me we both need to review our ideas about the world, Mrs Turner,' he told her seriously. The thought of her walled up in gloomy isolation made his heart ache as well as the rest of him.

'Maybe we do, but not now,' she told him as if she was humouring him. She rose from her chair to lean over him and he meekly allowed himself to be in pain and bone-weary and in dire need of her care and compassion. Tomorrow would be soon enough to restart his whole life and she still needed to be persuaded her plans were ridiculous. That sounded enough of a challenge for now and she was right, he was very tired.

Chapter Seven

'Did you sleep at all last night?' Darius demanded when he came downstairs and found the back door open and his sister outside. Marianne was sitting on the low wall that separated the house from the road to the farm, gazing at the view she had become very fond of during the short time they had lived here.

'Yes,' she said and carried on watching the sky lighten and listening to the chorus of birdsong because her brother had a gift for being silent and worming more out of her than she wanted to say. Even the birds seemed to pause as if waiting to hear more and that was nonsense, but far more effective than an open demand for information. 'My patient was very well behaved and slept for most of the night. He awoke about two and seemed perfectly rational, so we should not need to ask the sawbones to come back unless Lord Stratford becomes agitated and irrational. I am quite sure His Lordship is far too strong-willed to indulge in such weakness.'

'You still do not like him, then?'

Marianne paused to think about that question before she answered, 'He is well enough, I suppose. He must be very strong to withstand the ride he put himself through on his way here searching for Juno and he certainly has a stubborn nature to go with his physical prowess. No doubt he will want to put the discomforts of Owlet Manor behind him as soon as he can endure the journey to town or his nearest mansion to recover in style, so it does not really matter what I think.'

'I take it that is a "no", then?'

'I am trying to be neutral and fair-minded, if only you will let me. Maybe we did get off to a bad start, but he is a brave and determined man, even if he is stubborn as a donkey and will be a very difficult patient as soon as he begins to feel better. And given who we are and who *he* is, I am never likely to be better acquainted with him than I am now, so it hardly matters if I like him or not,' she said defensively.

Her brother did not need to know about the odd skip and thunder in her heartbeat when she had first set eyes on the bearlike and piratical-looking man standing on Miss Donne's doorstep. Nor the odd feeling she had when he had woken up in the night that they understood one another a little bit too well. She did not even want to think about her panic and bitter regret when she had run into the yard yesterday and it had looked as if Lord Stratford was seriously injured and might even die. A cold sense of dread had shivered through her when she had seen him lying unconscious at the base of that wall, but that was her secret and her worst fears were unfounded. Darius was not getting that out of her if he stayed silent and listening for the rest of the day. 'The kettle must have boiled by now. I will go and make tea,' she said to put paid to more uncomfortable questions.

'No, stay there and let me do something for you just this once,' Darius said, then left her brooding on the waking landscape and all the changes about to reorder her life, yet again.

They were too big to consider until she felt less tired, so she just sat in the strengthening sun and let it warm and soothe her before the power of it was too much to endure bareheaded. Now it felt reviving and reassuring and she allowed herself the luxury of revelling in the peace and quiet for a few precious minutes.

'Here you are,' Darius said softly and slipped the handle of one of the kitchen mugs into her hand, then went back inside to drink his own tea, as if he knew she wanted to be quiet and not think about anything much for a few moments at the beginning of another busy day.

He probably wanted to do the same himself, but his thoughts would be of Fliss and the new life they were about to begin together in this lovely old house. If anyone deserved a peaceful life and a happy marriage, it was Darius. Fliss needed a proper home as well, so this place would be perfect for her, and Marianne only envied them because she remembered how it felt to love someone as surely and completely as they loved one another now they had finally admitted it.

If only Daniel was here to share this lovely summer morning with her; if only he had lived to find such a peaceful home with her after the war was over, even if theirs would have been far more humble than Owlet Manor. He would have come with her to help Darius sort this lovely old place and its run-down farms out first and she knew Darius missed Daniel's energy and optimism as well. It would have been such fun with Daniel here to laugh with, she thought as tears blurred her eyes.

She shook her head and refused to live in Might Have Been Land because it was such a dangerous place to be that you could forget it was not real if you were not careful. She needed to get up and do whatever came next instead of sitting about regretting a future denied her by Daniel's death. The sneaky idea that she now had to regret the one she could never have with a nobleman like Alaric, Lord Stratford, as well crept into her head and made her frown. She only met him this time yesterday; that idea was not only sneaky, it was downright impossible.

Darius surprised her by coming back outside and sitting next to her with a very serious expression, as if he had tried to leave her in peace but whatever he had to say was too urgent to put off. 'We want you to stay, Nan. Fliss and I agree we cannot live without you and, before you say no to me without even thinking about it, she asked me to tell you she has always wanted a sister and will be very hurt if you refuse to stay at Owlet Manor because she will be living here as well.'

'Oh, well, that clinches the matter,' she said with a wry smile.

'I am serious and so is she, Marianne. We need you and this was never about finding work for you until the house was its proper self again. It was built for a family and we have always mattered to one another, you and I, but we do so even more after everything we saw and did in Portugal and Spain. I want this to be your home and Viola's as well, when we can finally persuade her to stop working for that rogue Marbeck and join us.'

'Even if she did she would rather find another post than become an idle lady paying calls and fascinating all the local beaux. It is your dream for all three of us to live under the same roof again, Darius, but it is not going to come true. It is a wonderful one and shows what a good man you are under your annoying elder-brother ways, but you have a true love to share this lovely old place with now and must stop worrying about your sisters. Get on with living the life you can have with Fliss and I wish you so very happy, Darius, but sooner or later I must move on as well. Viola has her own road to travel and neither of us wants to intrude on your new lives as man and wife.'

'I will never stop trying to change Viola's mind while she is in Sir Harry Marbeck's employ,' Darius said grimly.

Marianne wondered if he was thinking of galloping to Gloucestershire and demanding their little sister pack her bags and join them at Owlet Manor straight away. 'The more you rant and rave about the man, the less she will do as you want, Darius,' she warned. 'You ought to know Viola is as obstinate as both of us put together by now.'

'Aye, you are right,' he said with a gusty sigh, 'but please don't insist on going away as well, Nan,' he added as if it would hurt him. Trust him to know using his nickname for her from her childhood would sway her as much as she was willing to be swayed.

'I will stay long enough to help you and Fliss get this fine old place in good order for the wedding, but after that I must find something else to do, Darius. You know I cannot bear to be idle and Fliss already loves this house and will soon learn to run it with the help of some good servants and all the modern refinements you two can afford now she is rich. It will be a lovely, gracious old home for you and Fliss to raise your family and the last thing you need is your sisters here to argue and interfere at every turn. You know very well we would do so as soon as the first gloss of us all being a family again had worn off because neither of us is a meek and biddable female who would tactfully fade into the background.'

'You never stand still long enough to fade into anything,' he argued.

'I cannot, Darius,' she said seriously because she knew he would not let her laugh this off and he would argue with her every step of the way if she did not make him realise she was determined to leave. 'I need to be busy. I need it as much as Fliss needs to have her own home and I think she needs it very badly. It sounds as if she could never call anywhere home for very long as a child so she must have a place of her own to love and look after without me here to interfere.'

'I think you know us both a little too well, Little Sister,' he said with a heavy sigh, as if he did not think it a very good quality.

'I know how it feels to love as strongly and truly as you two do, now you have finally admitted it and thank goodness for that.'

'Aye, we have and we do,' he said with a far-off look in his eyes as he stared down the road to Broadley where his lover was sleeping without him.

'The sooner you two are wed and left to get on with being besotted with each other in peace, the better, then,' Marianne told him with a knowing smile and he just shrugged and grinned back at her. Loving Fliss had given him his true self back after those hard years on campaign. She would have to thank her sister-in-law-to-be for that even if she didn't already like her very much indeed for her own sake as well as his.

Yelverton and his sister must have been living more or less alone here for too long to worry that anyone could hear their murmured conversations. The narrow windows that actually opened must have been left wide to stop this room becoming stifling and even through the shutters Alaric could hear most of what they said in the stillness of yet another dawn. Listening shamelessly distracted him from his ills as he lay here like a log in the otherwise darkened room and he was not even ashamed of himself. He could not prop himself up to watch the sky lighten and doubted he could hold a book without flinching even if his battered brain could concentrate and he had enough light to read it. He needed to lie still to avoid jarring the bruise on the back of his head and making the confounded headache start up again.

So what else was there for him to do but lie here and eavesdrop? he concluded tetchily.

He flinched at the thought of the pain if he rolled his head the wrong way, but thank heavens the relentlessly pounding headache of last night had abated—as long as he did nothing foolish to start it off again. In the middle of the night he had been too preoccupied with worrying about his sanity and Mrs Marianne Turner to care about the boredom of recovery from a head wound. He hated the idea of being an invalid already and he was not even a day into it yet. How long did it take to be certain the danger of concussion and further damage was over, then? And when would he be able to walk or ride out in the pure light of early morning again?

He shuddered at the very thought of doing the latter just yet. Not that he was afraid to get back on a decent horse instead of the bad-tempered nag he had ridden yesterday. His brother had taught him to get back on a horse as soon as he fell off it as a boy and he had learned not to fear them. Horses were tricky creatures, much like people really in their likes and dislikes, diverse characters and strengths and weaknesses. On the whole he preferred horses and dogs to people now he lay here and thought about it—they were generally better tempered and a lot more reliable.

Except listening to the brother and sister talking about possible futures outside his window had made him think about people he could like. They were obviously very close and seemed to understand one another better than they probably wanted to be understood. He missed his brother so badly when he looked back at the one person who had made an effort to understand a scrubby brat seven years younger than the charmed heir to their father's title and lands. George had always done his best for his annoying little brother and Yelverton and Marianne's dilemma as they faced the truth that his marriage would mean she must move on touched him as he had not let himself be touched for far too long. Maybe there was something he could do to help them both. He might not be able to follow up on his instant attraction to the lovely Mrs Turner, but the spark of an idea had come into his aching head as he listened to their conversation.

'Uncle Alaric?' Juno's voice whispered from the doorway.

'Juno?' he asked foolishly because who else could it be with Yelverton and his sister communing with the rising sun outside and no sign of any indoor servants to be seen? He rolled his head on to the bruise when he tried to look at her and bit back a pained gasp so as not to frighten her away. 'Come in here where I can see you,' he said more harshly than he meant to because of the pain thundering through his head like a steam hammer as he rolled away from that side and sighed with relief. 'It hurts to twist round and peer at you when you stand over there,' he explained and hoped she would excuse so much more than one barked order when he was in pain. He held his breath and prayed silently she would forget to be afraid of him so they could start again.

'Sorry,' she said softly and came to the foot of the bed so he could see her as clearly as he was allowed to see anything in this shadowy old room. She looked so much paler than he remembered and thin with it. His heart twisted with self-loathing as he took in all he and his mother had done to the unfortunate girl between them with the Dowager's repellent scheming and his neglect.

'Do not apologise to me, Juno,' he said. 'I have done nothing to deserve it.' He heard the anguish in his own voice and was ashamed he could not find the strength to hide it for her sake.

'No, you do deserve it, Uncle Alaric, and I am so very sorry. I have been a widgeon about my come out and so many other things since. I am supposed to be grown up. I should have argued about going to London even when Grandmama insisted it was high time I made my debut and you agreed with her because other girls do it at my age and actually enjoy it. If I had told you how much I dreaded it, I know you would not have made me go. And I should have written to you the moment Grandmama tried to bullock me into marrying that horrid old man. So you see, none of this would have happened if I was braver. You would not be hurt so badly after riding all that way to find me and when you got here I just told you to go away.'

'That was not your fault and you did steel yourself to go to London when you did not want to go and you refused to marry that fat rogue and I am proud of you even if you are not. It took great courage to run away when the Dowager tried to force your hand. I cannot even imagine how terrified you must have been when you had to set out on such a journey alone and you got all the way here with no money left as well, Jojo. All in all, I cannot think of any girl I ever met who has more courage than you.'

His imagination painted a picture of a much younger Marianne flying from her safe home at whatever vicarage she came from to find, then wed, her gallant soldier. Perhaps there was one girl who had been as brave, if not braver, than Juno when she set out to find Miss Grantham and ask for sanctuary then, but as he had not met Marianne at that age he was still telling the absolute truth. He did not want a picture in his head of how delicious and headstrong and innocently determined Miss Marianne Yelverton must have been when she set her heart on her late husband, come what may. The woman she was now plagued him badly enough without adding another layer of temptation to the mix.

'A bolder person would have got her own way without needing to run,' Juno objected, so he had to push the tempting image of a young and dreamy-eyed Marianne aside to concentrate on Juno. Had she always been so resistant to praise and how could he not know something so important about his own niece?

'I doubt it and stop finding yourself less than everyone else you know. There is no bravery in doing something you do not fear and I like you far better than the usual simpering debutante with an abacus where her heart should be,' he said and at least Juno was never going to be the sort of ruthless husband hunter he had learned to avoid since inheriting George's title and lands at seventeen. 'You are kind-hearted and clever and far nicer, as well as a lot more interesting, than those preening girls with so little to preen about. I should have done better by you than I have until now, but you must believe me, Juno, no sane person I have ever come across is as certain of themselves as you seem to think they are.'

'Not even you?'

'Especially not me and if you promise to

try harder to fight your demons in the future, then I will do the same with mine,' he offered with a wry smile.

'I doubt you have ever had a shy moment in your entire life, Uncle Alaric.'

'I expect I could surprise you with one or two, but we all have our own worries and shortcomings, Jojo,' he said and he had certainly learnt a lot about his own dark places since he set out on his frantic quest to find her.

'When I saw you lying there hurt I felt...' Juno hesitated and Alaric willed her to go on. He wanted better for her, wanted her to live well in her own skin and know she always had a right to be listened to, even if he had not been very good at it in the past. 'Furious with myself,' she went on as if she had to physically push the words out of her mouth. 'You came all the way from Paris to Broadley, then out here to Owlet Manor in order to find me, although you were obviously so tired after riding all that way that you could barely stand upright when you got here. And you only came to make sure I was truly unharmed by the storm and the journey and having to walk the rest of the way here from Worcester after I was robbed. Then, when you got here, I hid away from you like a timid little child and refused to even meet your eyes across a room.'

'I was the adult and you really were a child when this all began. I should never have left you with your grandmother after your father died. I ought to have done what I wanted to at the time and found a kindly older lady to help you settle so you could live with me at Stratford Park instead of at the Dower House. Not that the Dowager has spent much time there in the last few years, but I should never have let her persuade me I was not fit to care for you and you needed her. Apparently the world would think it odd if you did not live with her and that should not have mattered one jot beside your happiness and well-being.'

'I would rather have been with you and I was very glad Grandmama spent most of her time in London,' Juno said with the ghost of a smile.

'So was I,' he confided with a wan smile back. 'I should have realised she did not love you years ago, but I was blinded by the fact she adored your father and thought she must love you as well. I should have been old enough to stop worrying what people would think if you lived with me instead.'

'I do not think she likes either of us very much.' Juno's smile was more certain now and he managed to find a better one in return.

'No, but I really do love you, Juno, and you are going to grow very tired of me telling you so for the rest of your life to make up for being such a fool until now. I promise you I will not keep my feelings to myself from now on.'

'Things could get very complicated if you wear your heart on your sleeve all the time, Uncle Alaric.'

'Aye, you are quite right, niece. Then I had best limit myself to being open with you and anyone else I somehow manage to love or like. The rest of the world can be excused knowing exactly what I think of it.'

'Considering how little patience you have with some parts of it that would be as well.'

'True—and I think you know me a little bit too well.'

'I watch people a lot, even when I feel too shy to join in.'

'Then we must find more of them you feel happy to engage with or you will soon become a cynic.'

'No, I love Miss Grantham and already like Mrs Turner and Mr Yelverton very much. I even quite like you at times, Uncle Alaric, although obviously you do not count since you are family and obliged to like me anyway,' she teased him, this girl he had been so desperate to find on his way here it seemed to have torn open his closed heart and remade him.

His mother's cold indifference at best and hatred at worst, then George's tragically premature death in the hunting field had made him a puzzled and lonely youth. He shut that boy away and concentrated on being Lord Stratford, but it was about time he came out from behind his title and learnt to be himself—if only he knew who that was. He would have to learn to ignore his inner sceptic if he wanted to make Juno's life better and stop guarding himself against strong emotions for the rest of his life. And he was tired of being the lord who walked alone. His fine plan to wed Miss Grantham and keep his viscountess at a distance would have been a disaster, so it was as well she came here and found true love instead.

'Obviously I am very relieved about that,' he said and might have said more, but sensed Mrs Turner was nearby even before she came into the room so quietly he wondered how he had been so certain. This odd awareness of her kept his senses constantly on the alert. His heart began to race when she was within a hundred yards and he had strained his ears for every murmured word she had said to Yelverton under his window this morning, as if he could store them up like treasure against the time he must leave here and go on his lonely way.

Maybe that scheme he had been mulling over would mean not having to leave her behind when he went. It might be a bittersweet torture to be close to a woman so beguilingly unaware of her own attractions and not be able to do anything about it, but something told him he would regret it if he put his own comfort first and ignored her sad dilemma.

He still hoped she would not gauge his heart-beat now because she would have the saw-bones out here as fast as his horse would go.

'Ah, there you are, Juno,' she said and per-haps it was as well. He was more than de-lighted to be on good terms with his niece again, but he still felt as if a half-dozen horses had galloped over him yesterday. Strong emo-tions were exhausting, he decided. No won-der he had avoided them since his brother died.

'I meant to sit quietly by Uncle Alaric's bed until he woke up, but he was awake when I got here,' Juno said sheepishly as she faced Marianne's sceptical gaze.

'She has done me good, Mrs Turner,' Alaric defended her and it was true, or it would be tomorrow morning when he woke up feeling better *and* fairly certain his niece was not going to flee as soon as he was well enough to get up.

'I am sure your company has done your uncle more good than any tonic I have to hand, Juno, but my brother is about to come up here to help your uncle wash and shave. I doubt His Lordship will want either of us nearby while he curses his injuries and very likely my brother up hill and down dale.'

'Almost certainly him as well,' Alaric muttered grumpily, but his dislike of the man was only show by now. He had already forgiven the man for stealing his would-be fiancée. One day he might thank him for loving a young woman he admired for her learning and grace and courage, but did not love. If not for Yelverton, he would have to consider himself bound by his carefully considered offer for the admirable Miss Grantham. Something told him neither of them would have been very happy shackled together for life and they had both had a lucky escape.

Chapter Eight

After all that cursing and discomfort, her patient was so pale and exhausted Marianne insisted on leaving him to sleep despite his insistence he was not tired and had already slept for hours. He did so for several more, so at least that was half a day over without him trying to get out of bed. She had sensed his restless energy on the other side of the door before she even set eyes on him yesterday, so she knew it would only get more difficult to keep him quiet when he felt better. Watching him sleep in the shadowed room now, she was surprised to discover that she hated seeing him brought low like this. It was like a bird of prey being chained to a post or hooded when to her mind they should always fly free.

Fanciful nonsense, she told herself as she

turned to go so he could sleep boredom away a little longer.

Hopefully his body had more sense than the rest of him and it would force him to rest and heal before he made any more ridiculous demands of it. Yet he had proved that he did not listen when he had pushed himself to exhaustion on his way here. It was such a fine and powerful male body as well and it seemed a crying shame to abuse it with his usual lordly bullheadedness.

'Mrs Turner?' he murmured even as she turned to leave.

'I am sorry I woke you.'

'Everybody seems to be sorry for me today, one way or the other,' he said and was that really a self-deprecating smile or just a trick of the shadows in a darkened room? If it was, then how dare he have a sense of humour to make him seem more human than he was yesterday? 'Even your brother apologised for hurting me just now, so he thinks I am as fragile as glass and was trying to be kinder than I probably deserve.'

'Do you still have the headache, my lord?'

'Not unless I roll about on the lump on the back of my head.'

'Then do you think you could endure a little light if I open the shutters slightly?' she asked to try and gauge how sensitive to light he was and if she ought to worry about him more than she already was. If there was a lingering chance of concussion it should have shown by now, but she was determined to keep him in bed for another day just in case she was wrong.

'Gladly. I would like to see even a hint of today since I seem to be sleeping so much of it away it feels like a waste of a fine summer day.'

'You *are* injured, Lord Stratford. You must take care until we are sure your head injury is less serious than the doctor feared. I knew you were going to be a difficult patient the moment you started to feel a little better,' she said with her back to him as she let in a small shaft of curious sunlight now it had moved up the sky and would not shine directly into his eyes.

She tried hard to pretend he was only a man in need of a little compassion and not in any way special as she drifted about his bedchamber, tidying little details of the room Darius had no time to worry about. If she tried hard enough, she could forget Lord Stratford possessed strength and character as well as too much money for his own good—oh, and that wretched title as well. Mother Nature had been generous with her gifts when he was born and Marianne wondered if the lady was hell-bent on mischief when she gave him energy and presence as well as an unforgettable face, even if she had withheld classically handsome features. The man was too definite for such smooth good looks, but by the time you realised that it was too late—he had already remade handsome and the rest into also-rans.

'Who, me?' he answered as if he would never dream of being awkward or lordly and she almost laughed.

She added charm, when he chose to use it, to that list of unfair ways Lord Stratford was unforgettable and frowned to make it clear that tactic would not get round her any better than a brusque series of orders. 'Yes, you. It is in your best interest to rest until your head is better and trying to charm your way down-stairs before you are ready to leave this room will not get you anywhere.'

'I shall have to confound you and endure it like a gentleman then, or is that your plan, Mrs Turner? You point out how awkward I am likely to be so I will play the perfect invalid to show you how wrong you are. Is that how you keep ugly customers like me in order?'

'I don't know, I have never had to deal with one quite as ugly as you before, Lord Stratford,' she lied smoothly, but this time he grinned at her as if he knew it was untrue. He thought he had her measure and that felt far too dangerous. The last thing she wanted was him knowing what she really thought of him. If he knew she had tried to sleep earlier, after far too many wearisome days and nights of worrying over Juno and then him, and failed because of him, he would know he had the advantage and play on it to get his own way. Even closing her eyes and trying to nap had been a mistake, she reminded herself.

She turned away from him again and frowned down at the short stretch of garden where the house backed on to the road to the farm and stables through the sliver of a gap in the shutters. She had thought it was prudent to allow him this so he would not get out of bed and fling them wide as soon as her back was turned. Yet as soon as she tried to relax she was haunted by silly images of him awake and aware under her searching hands, instead of unconscious and worryingly still as he was yesterday when she frantically explored his body for injuries. He had such a honed and muscular body under his once-splendid clothes as well.

She did not usually care how a man would look naked, not since she lost Daniel and thought she would never want to be intimate with a man ever again. Yet even now her fingers twitched involuntarily as if they were longing for the feel of him under them again, so she eyed them as if they had turned traitor. They still yearned to explore his firm satin skin over honed muscles and a flat belly she had been certain no aristocrat would possess, until she searched almost every inch of him for hurts she winced at finding, although she kept telling herself he was nothing to her.

'If that does not work, I shall just have to find another way to stop you doing yourself permanent damage by doing too much too soon,' she said and from the hot dare in his mesmerising blue eyes he had heard the mistake in that sentence just as she did as soon as it was out of her mouth. No, she would not be joining him in that bed to keep him there until he was well enough to get up and start ordering the world again. 'A sleeping draught, perhaps, or maybe I could get Darius to knock you out with a cudgel,' she added.

A fiery blush still stung her cheeks at the image of them in bed together with her doing all sorts of wrong and inventive things to keep him there. She cursed herself for that give-away flush of hot colour and he could hardly miss it when there was not much else to look at in this bare bedchamber. She had only just got it clean and had had a new mattress brought in when he needed it so urgently. All the extra comforts she was planning to add hadn't seemed important. She would have another chair or two brought up so the others could sit with him and keep him amused. And she needed to consult Fliss about adding a rug and some furniture. If Lord Stratford felt more comfortable, he might be less restless and less inclined to run before he could walk on that damaged ankle. There, she had almost forgotten to be conscious of him as a man while she did her best to reduce his stay here to a domestic detail.

'I can think of better reasons to be a good patient,' he told her with a mock leer and an altogether too-disarming grin.

There was still a hot promise in his gaze so she avoided it and frowned at a fresh cobweb instead. There could never be anything between a lord and a humble widow they would not be ashamed of afterwards. 'I doubt you know how to be patient in any sense of the word, my lord,' she forced herself to say lightly.

'And I am trying so hard to be humble,' he told her half-seriously and she nearly laughed. She could not imagine a less humble man if she ran through a list of the hot-headed and entitled officers she had met from the Duke of Wellington downwards.

'It could take a lifetime,' she argued and he smiled as if he knew he was naturally arrogant and impatient, but he was less lordly and very human in private.

'I will need a lot of help, then,' he said huskily and all the images in her head earlier were hot in his piercingly blue eyes as he gazed back at her.

Even his mouth looked firm and inviting as the notion of what that help might involve sang between them. He was an invalid, for goodness' sake. And even when he was well he would still be a viscount. Before she went away again she ought to check the bandages on his wrist and ankle were tight enough, but not cutting into him, except being so close to him right now seemed a bad idea. She almost wished he would go back to being the arrogant and objectionable nobleman she met yesterday. It would be so much easier to treat him with cool and impersonal efficiency, then go back to getting the house ready for a wedding.

With any luck he would be well enough to be very gently driven to Broadley and the best inn in town very soon. He could live there in comfort until he was ready to be driven home in his own beautifully sprung carriage.

And if she kept on putting his money, rank and privilege between them maybe she would stop finding him so attractive and powerfully male, even when he was lying there in Darius's nightshirt and should look less than his usual overconfident self.

She heard a stir down in the yard and thank goodness for a distraction. Now she could be taken up with whoever was out there instead of him *and* she would not have to get that close to the man without Darius here to take away the intimacy of it.

'I wonder who that can be?' she said, with a *tut-tut* to tell him she did not have time or inclination for visitors. Really, she would be glad to see anyone who would drag her away from his side and break this ridiculous spell he seemed to have cast over her at first sight. She still loved Daniel and she always would, so of course she did not want another man and she *really* did not want to want a lord like this one.

'I have no idea,' he said, 'but at least you can walk over to the window and see for yourself.'

'Hmm, well, I cannot see why anyone would

be… Oh, my word,' she gasped as a team of dray horses came properly into view, then the dray itself appeared, loaded with boxes and all sorts of odd items as if half a house full of furniture and trappings were on the move, but what on earth were they doing here?

'For goodness' sake, woman, will you stop peering at whoever is out there and tell me what is going on?' His Lordship snapped from the bed in angry frustration and there he was again, Alaric the Pirate; barking orders from his sickbed. Good, he should make her temper flare and stop her having silly and overheated ideas about Alaric the man.

'If I knew that I might tell you,' she said and turned back from the window with a frown and a stern dare not to even lift his head off his pillow, let alone attempt to get out of bed and see for himself. 'There is a dray loaded with boxes and bags and furniture drawing up outside, Lord Stratford, and I have to suppose that the driver and his mate have been directed to the wrong place to deliver it since I did not order a single stick of it. I had better go downstairs and send them to wherever they are supposed to be going with it all.'

'Ah, apparently your friend Miss Donne is even more efficient than I thought.'

'What on earth can all that stuff have to do with her?'

'The lady obviously has the good sense to worry about your reputation even if you do not, Mrs Turner. If you continue to stay here without a duenna of some sort now I am in the house, your good name will be in shreds.'

'I do not have a good name for the gossips to destroy, so it does not matter what they think of me,' she said. The bitterness in her own voice shocked her. The snide remarks about ladies who wilfully married below their station she had had to pretend not to hear in Bath must have hurt her more than she realised at the time, numbed as she still thought she was by Daniel's death.

The sound of it made Lord Stratford frown, then look lordly and impatient. 'It matters to me,' he said so mildly she felt the sting of his temper more than if he had shouted at her.

A little bit of warmth and caring about her well-being was in there as well as impatience and that might have disarmed her, if she was not already furious about the silly conventions he was worrying about a lot more than she wanted him to. If such empty notions of propriety had made a friend rush here, she would far rather she stayed away. And she did not have time for any more distractions right now, or enough cleared bedrooms to receive them if they intended to stay as that wagonload of furniture and luggage made it look as if they might. 'It does not matter as much as a snap of my fingers to me,' she told him defiantly.

'You were born a lady whether you like it or not, Mrs Turner, and I do not think your brother would thank me for calling him less than a gentleman now. You are still Yelverton's sister and he has the role of lord of the manor to keep up whether you like it or not. You have to be concerned for your good name if you do not want your family suffering from your lack of one by association.'

That nagging piece of grit in her oyster made her want to blaze fury back at him and tell him he had never been more wrong in his life, but he was quite right, drat him. 'I know,' she admitted with a heavy sigh.

Her sister Viola might live in a respectable house several miles away from Chantry Old Hall with her charges and a stern maiden aunt of Sir Harry Marbeck's, but she was still in Sir Harry's employ and vulnerable to gossip about her family. For Viola's sake and for Darius and Fliss's she had to pay lip service to the conventions. Doubtless Fliss and Darius would soon add another generation of Yelvertons to the mix and the lid would be screwed down on Marianne's dreams of an independent life once and for all. So she might have to care about things she had left behind with a sigh of relief when she married Daniel, but that did not mean she must like it.

'I cannot undo the past even if I wanted to and I do not, Lord Stratford,' she told him defiantly. 'I do not regret my runaway marriage. As I was not ashamed of my husband while he was alive, I am certainly not going to be now.'

'Why should you be?' he said with a quieter

challenge. 'Do you expect me to think less of your late husband because he was born in a more humble bed than you or I? He must have been a brave and honourable man for you to want to marry him in the first place and I respect such men wherever I meet them.'

He sounded offended by her assumption he would not, so she supposed she ought to stop making them. She had secretly accused him of prejudice from the moment their eyes met on that doorstep and he had mistaken her for the maid and her fury with him for that misstep felt far too personal now. She shook her head at her own stupidity, but he took it as disagreement with him and impatience flashed in his eyes as he shot a challenge back at her.

'Perhaps you ought to think harder about which of us is most inclined to rush to judgement, Mrs Turner,' he said with a hint of disgust that made her squirm.

'What you think of me is immaterial. I must go and find out what is going on down there and if you have any sense you will go back to sleep,' she told him brusquely, trying to pretend his accusation did not sting. What looked like a hired gig had arrived outside now and she saw Fliss draw the horse to a neat halt, so at least her attempt to teach her friend to drive over the last few weeks had paid off.

'Curse it, we are not done,' Lord Stratford said as she turned away from her vantage point to leave him to his solitude with what she told herself was a sigh of relief.

'We are as far as I am concerned,' she told him and at least in his current state she could walk away from an argument with him. If he was his usual self, she would probably not get halfway across the room before he stood in her way to stop her going and make her listen to his opinion of her. He might even kiss her to be certain of her attention and that was an indignity she must not even think of. So she did nothing else but wonder how it would feel to be kissed by His Lordship while she ran downstairs as if the devil was on her tail.

How fortunate that Miss Donne, Fliss and all those trappings were waiting outside to distract her from impossible fantasies. The very idea of Lord Stratford kissing her until she forgot all the differences between them and sighed for him like a dizzy schoolgirl was unthinkable. It was high time she got it right out of her head and went on with real life.

Chapter Nine

'That was well done, Defford,' Alaric muttered disgustedly as he listened to Marianne hurry away. Now he was shut up here with his wretched body aching in every bone and sinew and his head hurt like blazes. No use trying to get up and stagger after her to apologise and explain himself better. 'The lady must be feeling so much better about her hard lot in life now, you infernal idiot.'

Unfortunately for him the fantasy he had of her sleepy eyed and sated in his bed while he was drifting in and out of sleep yesterday was impossible. Mrs Turner was a lady, whether she wanted to be one or not, so he could not ask her to be his mistress. And the idea of her life being picked over and sniffed at by the Dowagers if he married her made him shudder. Only if they were deeply in love would there be any point risking all the gossip about her late husband and how on earth she had managed to hook his exact opposite the second time around. Marianne's defiance of the social conventions when she ran away to wed a so-called common soldier would outrage the high sticklers and make her the target of all sorts of wrong-headed speculation. He did not particularly want to have his sanity questioned by his peers either and he was not in love with the woman, he merely admired her beauty and her spirit and her fiery determination and her lithe and lovely figure and… Hmm, that was an awful lot of *and*s.

Never mind—admiration was not love so they were still impossible for one another and that was good. She would laugh if she knew what a sad state of longing and yearning he had got himself into when he met her sceptical blue eyes for the first time. He was very tired at the time and she was all sleepy eyed and ruffled, so of course she had looked delicious and desirable and like the embodiment of all the dreams he had refused to have as the youthful quarry of most of the husband hunters in the polite world.

As a suddenly desirable young lord instead of a younger son, at first it had taken all his energy to escape the traps laid for a single viscount in possession of all his limbs and teeth. So he had dared not dream of meeting an enchantress one night in Mayfair and falling head over heels in love lest she turn out to be a younger version of his famously beautiful mother. It was too dangerous to dream back then. Since he had acquired enough town bronze to evade the little darlings so eager to be a viscountess they would have taken him even if he had two horns and a tail, he had become too cynical to dream about anything much at all.

He could not accuse Marianne of trying to enchant him when she was obviously not at all pleased to see him that first time, but he contrarily wished she would, then he could stop thinking his way around this feral attraction and let himself just feel for once in his life. He wanted her to look at him as if she could not help tingling with sensual awareness whenever he was near.

He knew an affair was impossible and he could not ruin a woman who had risked so much for the love of a very different man even if she wanted him to. Yet he tried to define the faint scent she had left behind in this bare old room and knew if she felt anything like as itchy and tempted and frustrated about him as he did about her they would be in deep trouble. He would get over it; he knew how to lock up his emotions, but if hers were engaged he could not fight them both. Her refusal to see sense last time she had loved made her dangerous. Except the very idea of being loved so much she stopped caring who he was and did it anyway seemed magnificent and so much bigger than anything he had ever dared hope for. Just as well she did not love him, then.

He snuffled like a hound and managed to pick a few elements of Mrs Marianne Turner out of the air—hmm, there was rose water to start with and something herbal and sharper underneath it…rosemary, perhaps, or lemon balm. Or was that the scent clinging to the pillow under his head after it was dried by fresh air and summer sun? Not a fancy preparation for a lady's complexion or a faint drift of expensive perfume anyway—he could not imagine her spending a single penny more than necessary on her toilette. Perhaps those faint, clean scents came from a home-made washing ball. Yes, that seemed a good fit. From the clean and tidy but spartan state of this room he concluded Yelverton had naught to spare for many of the things Alaric took for granted. Yelverton would still lack them until he wed Miss Grantham, so the man's sister must have worked her fingers to the bone to provide as many as could be had by hard work.

Alaric would be angry on her behalf if he had not realised she was so stubborn she probably insisted on doing everything herself here, even if Yelverton offered to hire someone to do the rough work. She would tell him to put the money into his land and livestock and let her work her way through this grand but neglected old house one room at a time. Alaric hated the idea of her doing everything except scrub floors and chop firewood and he would not put it past her to do even that if her brother let her.

He reminded himself of the reality of his life and the vast distance in station yawning between them, even if she was not still grieving for another man. He was interested in Marianne Turner as a potential companion for his niece in the real world where they both had to live. Getting her to see herself as a lady of gentle birth again was the first part of finding Juno someone she could feel at ease with now Miss Grantham was going to be married to Yelverton and far too busy with him and his tumbledown old house to take on any more responsibility. He could tell from that muttered conversation this morning Marianne was in a dilemma about the future and it seemed like killing two birds with one stone to offer her the post of Juno's companion to save her from being preyed on or exploited by some ruthless future employer.

His hands tightened into fists again at the very thought of some unscrupulous seducer setting eyes on the unaware but lovely Mrs Turner and deciding to get her into his bed by fair means or foul. A jag of pain shot through his injured wrist and reminded him he was lying here like a useless block and in no fit state to hit a rake preying on an honourable man's honourable widow. A widow who did not sound in the least bit receptive to a potential employer who had his own hot thoughts about her he would learn to live with. He was not important; it was his niece's happiness that mattered now. And even Juno seemed to have abandoned him for more exciting people and events. He allowed himself to feel a little aggrieved about that while getting ready to resist Mrs Turner's vibrant looks, natural charm and humour and all her other attractions for Juno's sake.

Alaric eyed the narrow shaft of sunlight slowly working its way across the room and letting him know there were much better things to do outside if only he dared get out of bed. He huffed out a sigh of self-pity and gloomily counted out the least number of days he could spend in this old-fashioned, unexciting bedchamber before he dared risk defying orders and felt even worse. 'Best go to sleep again and while away the time that way, Stratford,' he ordered himself, 'and make sure you do not dream of a sleepy-eyed siren who wants you as urgently as you want her this time.' If willpower could get him well and out of here and Juno happy with the right companion to help her face the world, he had best march it out right away.

Marianne saw the doctor out of the front door, waved a distracted farewell then sat down on one of the ancient oak benches in the grand entrance porch with a heavy sigh. There was nothing she could do to keep Lord Stratford in bed and safely out of the way now all danger of him suffering lasting damage if he stirred had been officially pronounced over and done. She hardly had time to sit and dream of an uncomplicated life without any viscounts in it when she heard the sound of His Lordship's uneven footsteps on the stone floor behind her.

She got up to eye the man with disfavour and tried to ignore the skip in her heartbeat at seeing him fully dressed and almost his arrogant self again. He was easily as handsome as the devil and could be every bit as dangerous if she let herself be beguiled by him. 'I thought you were supposed to use a stick,' she told him grumpily.

'Find me one and I will.'

'Stay there, then,' she ordered him sharply

and went to raid her late great-uncle's store of them in his still-untouched study. Tempted by the mischievous image of a lord hobbling about the place with the aid of a roughly fashioned one from a country hedgerow, she snatched up a silver-mounted gentleman's walking cane Uncle Hubert must have kept for best instead, before Lord Stratford limped in here in her wake. 'Here,' she said, thrusting the cane at him as she turned round to march back into the hall and found him only a few steps behind her. 'Do you never stay where you are put?' she asked crossly. She would never see him as a rich and entitled gentleman if he kept getting so close she could almost feel him breathe.

'Not if I can help it,' he said unrepentantly, swirled his new prop with his good hand and nodded approvingly as if he was surprised about not being given a hedge stick as well. 'Now tell me what is to do here?'

'Nothing as far as you are concerned,' she told him with a frown—what was a still-injured viscount intending to do in another man's house?

'I never could abide doing that.'

'Me neither,' she said unwarily and saw him raise his eyebrows at such heartfelt agreement when they argued over most things.

'Perhaps we should stroll about the ground floor of your brother's house and take a look at what you Yelvertons laughingly call a garden. I need some exercise, you see, the doctor said so.'

'He said a little gentle walk would do your ankle no harm, not that you should stamp about the place ordering everyone about and getting in the way.'

'You do not know that I will,' he objected quite mildly and held out the elbow of his good arm for her to hold.

She placed her hand on it before her head could order the rest of her not to be so witless. 'I know you have been fretting for something to do and I heard you and Darius arguing about it while he was shaving you this morning,' she admitted.

'Did you, now—eavesdropping, Mrs Turner? How very unbecoming in a lady.'

'I told you, I am not—'

'And I believe I told you that you are very

much a lady, like it or not,' he interrupted before she could make her usual disclaimer.

'And Lord Stratford's word is law?' she carped, mostly because she did not like being ridden over roughshod and a little bit because she was far too conscious of him walking at her side. She could feel his firm muscles flex under her fingertips and there was this silly sense it was right to walk at his side and argue over what should happen next and how they were to bring it about.

'With you about to disagree I very much doubt it, but on important matters it is as well to be firm from the outset.'

'And if you say I am a genteel widow I shall be one whether I like it or not?'

'Precisely, so, as your brother and Miss Grantham seem determined to marry the moment the banns have been read, where are you planning to hold the wedding breakfast?' he said as if that was her sorted out so now it was time for the next item on his list.

'You two seem to have been confiding in one another like a pair of ageing spinsters.'

'We are the only males in a houseful of females, so we men must stick together. He tells me Miss Grantham wants to have the wedding breakfast here, so where are you planning to serve food and drink and what about this dancing your brother seems to be dreading so deeply I think he envies me a sore ankle as an excuse to escape it?'

'Does he, indeed?'

'Yes, he says he has two left feet.'

'I have to admit he is right—he would never have made a staff officer since the Beau always insisted they could dance as well as they ride.'

'I dare say Miss Grantham will love him anyway.'

'I dare say.'

'So where are you intending to hold all this dissipation at such short notice?'

'The dining room and drawing room are the obvious places,' she said, not quite ready to admit the two large rooms were beyond her in the scant weeks Darius and Fliss were prepared to wait before they married.

'Hmm, difficult in three weeks, but not impossible,' he told her after they had inspected the untouched rooms.

She had done her best to ignore them ever since she and Darius arrived in Herefordshire, although Darius would have been quite happy for her to put all her effort into them, but then he would have expected her to sit in the drawing room and receive his neighbours. She had far better things to do and no intention of being disapproved of by another set of genteel gossips after her experiences in Bath. So she concentrated on kitchens and bedchambers and the smaller parlour and morning room once used by the family.

'As it is high summer, Miss Donne has suggested using lengths of muslin or gauze to make a pretend marquee and hide the smoke stains on the ceiling,' she explained as they stood in the once-grand dining room. 'And we can put flowers in front of the damaged wainscoting. Maybe the wedding guests will not look closely if the food is lavish and a good polish will hide a multitude of sins.'

'In here, perhaps, but not in the drawing room where there is no feast or wedding toasts to distract them.'

'Maybe after all those toasts they will not

care the chairs are old-fashioned and worn and the cushions and curtains moth-eaten.'

'Maybe not, but I owe your brother and Miss Grantham Juno's safety and well-being. They gave her a place to run to when she was desperate and a roof over her head when she got here. I can never thank them enough for being here for her when I was too far away to realise what was going on. Making sure their wedding is memorable for the right reasons feels like the best I can do to say thank you to them, with your help, of course. My people can help bring it about if you will supervise.'

'I know Darius will have already argued that you owe nothing.'

He stopped and frowned at the dust and neglect around them. 'This fine old place has been left to tumble down,' he said severely.

'Yes, and I know when I am being diverted from a scent, Lord Stratford,' she told him. 'And what people do you mean?'

'The servants at Stratford Park have been idle all summer so they might as well come here and make themselves useful before they forget how.'

'And why do I feel as if I am being presented with a fait accompli?'

'I have no idea,' he said. 'Perhaps we should look at the mess of weeds and brambles your brother calls a garden next,' he added and they were already on their way out of the open front door so here was another one.

'What about it?' she said with an annoyed glance at the wilderness all around them. 'And I do not think either of us would call it anything so grand.'

'If it is tamed, the wedding guests can wander round it.'

'Maybe it will be wet.'

'Oh, ye of little faith,' he teased her and somehow it was almost comfortable strolling along at his side as if she really were a lady.

It was so tempting to drift along in his powerful wake. 'You are a very managing man,' she told him curtly.

Chapter Ten

Alaric was doing so well at reining in his base instincts until he paid more attention to the rebellious glint in Marianne's eyes than where he was going. The tip of his cane slid on a patch of loose stones and quick as lightning she grabbed his arm, as if she thought he might break if she let him fall. He grasped her waist on an instinct he did not quite trust and told himself it was to steady them both. The novelty of being protected by a beautiful woman threatened all his resolutions not to kiss her, so he had to stop this before it got out of hand. He used his good leg to stop the slide and managed not to curse out loud in front of a lady, but however hard he tried to he could not make himself let her go.

'You must take more care,' she warned huskily.

'So must you,' he cautioned. He heard her breath stutter, then quicken. Her lips were parted and she licked them as if they suddenly felt dry and that was what really undid him. He was kissing her before his mind could scream no. It felt as if he had been starving for her mouth, her lips and her startled response as he deepened their kiss since the first moment he had laid eyes on her. And she gave herself up to their kiss as if this was what they were born for, so what had he been waiting for? *You*, an inner voice whispered.

With her lips soft yet demanding as they blotted out the world together, he felt as if they could do anything; be lovers; trust one another completely; be everything to one another. Heat and light and need shot through him and he groaned into her luxury of a mouth. He drew her closer, shaped the back of her head with shaking hands and opened his mouth on hers. And she met his tongue as he explored and teased hers—and that was the moment he took a step too far towards her and his stupid ankle slipped again.

This time he grabbed her close and shifted his balance on to his good leg to protect her from his clumsiness. He cursed himself for taking even the slightest risk with her. He should never have tried to kiss her on his first trip outside his spartan bedchamber in a week. He felt her stiffen and curve away from him even as they saved themselves from a tumble once again. Ah, yes, that was the truth of it; he should never have kissed her at all.

Breathless and flushed, she was even more delicious and desirable now she would not meet his gaze. When she tried to speak it looked as if words had deserted her. She shook her head and looked away. They had taken a huge step into intimacy, then a hasty jump back. He wanted to tell her he was glad *and* sorry for it, so he stood tense and silent instead. What an odd tableau if anyone could see them in this wilderness, but she was more important than who knew what and when.

He was going to live a very different life from his old one and to do it he had to renounce his best fantasy of Marianne love shot and heavy-eyed in his bed. She was a lady and the widow of a man who gave his life for his country. He wanted her to feel safe at

Stratford Park if she agreed to become Juno's companion and she was hardly likely to if she was afraid he would impose himself on her whenever they were alone.

'I am sorry,' he said stiffly. 'I promise you it will not happen again.'

'Good,' she managed to say at last.

Of course she agreed; why would she not? He was not a very impressive figure with a weak ankle, sore wrist and poor record as a human being. 'Please accept my sincere apology, Mrs Turner,' he asked as they stood several yards apart.

'I loved my husband, Lord Stratford,' she said, then eyed him warily as if he might be about to argue, given her fiery response to him in that fleeting, glorious moment before she recalled who she was kissing.

'I am sure you did, ma'am,' he said stiffly.

She shrugged and looked as if she still could not find the words to tell him how much less than the late Mr Turner he was. 'Don't call me ma'am,' she ordered him sharply instead.

'No, m—' he began, then hastily amended at her glare. 'Mrs Turner.'

Juno. Remember how much her happi-

ness matters, Stratford, he reminded himself sternly.

'I am not usually so clumsy,' he added.

'You have an injured ankle.'

'I am surprised you did not kick me in the other one and make it a pair.'

'I should have resisted your kiss and you should not have kissed me in the first place—that is the beginning and end of the matter. We must try to forget it ever happened.'

'Very well, if that is what you want,' he agreed. His inner idiot was jumping up and down, wanting to know where that much forgetfulness was going to come from. It did feel as if awareness of all they could be together was branded on his very soul by that hot and deliciously passionate kiss. No, he was a cold man at heart—he must be to have ridden away from London when Juno needed him. He was sure he could will all this heat and desire stone dead if he tried hard enough and she did, too.

'I do,' she asserted and they were in complete accord for once.

That was wonderful, but it seemed like a good idea to change the subject. 'Stratford

Park has been closed up for far too long,' he said and saw her puzzlement and a suspicion his wits might have been addled by that blow on his head after all.

'Indeed?' she said cautiously.

They both stared at what had once been a gravel walk covered in climbing roses as if seeing the chaos ahead of them was a lot easier than trying to explore places neither of them wanted to go. The air felt heavy with unsaid words as well as the scent of a last Bourbon rose gallantly blooming in its hard-fought-for corner. Most of the ironwork had collapsed under other roses grown wild and a mass of ivy and brambles added by Mother Nature. Luckily the wild disorder reminded him what they came out here to talk about.

'Even the servants sent to London to open up and run Stratford House for Juno's debut will have returned to Wiltshire by now,' he added, hanging on to his subject like a drowning man to lifeline.

'I hope they enjoyed their holiday.'

'If they did, it is well and truly over. Many of them are on their way here with my valet,' he confessed.

'Oh, really?' she said at last and sounded frostier than he had hoped.

He had best carry on explaining himself before she packed her bags and stormed off to stay with her parents. 'Your brother has agreed I can set them to work here instead of leaving them to argue endlessly at Stratford Park.'

'How easily led he has become since he fell in love,' she said coolly.

She was very good at making a man feel bad, wasn't she? He almost felt sorry for Turner facing his wife's wrath for some clumsy male misdemeanour. Except the man had her passionate love and Alaric was ashamed of being so jealous of a dead man. He wanted her sharp wits and hard-earned wisdom for Juno and he would just have to lock his inner satyr in the cellar and throw away the key when they got to Stratford Park.

'Love will do that to a man,' he said blandly. She looked so horrified when she took her eyes off the undergrowth it cost him an effort not to kiss her again. 'Or so I have been told,' he added to let her know he was not speaking from experience.

'Why?'

Why what? He shot her a sideways look and she was staring at the mess in front of them again and that was a relief, was it not? 'Why do I want to help Yelverton get this wreck in some sort of order for his wedding to my niece's former governess? Or why do people fall in love with one another when life would be so much simpler if they married for sense and a settled future?'

'Why help with all this, of course,' she said as if he was a fool to even ask.

'Miss Grantham was Juno's only real friend until recently. If not for her, Juno would have had nowhere to escape my mother's heartless plans for her.'

'She could have found you, my lord.'

'All the way across the Channel and on to Paris? I very much doubt it. I must pity her lack of a real home to flee to even if you do not.'

'That I do not. You would have made one wherever you happened to be if she only had the maturity to confide in you. Indeed, I doubt you would have gone in the first place if she had admitted how terrified she was of her grandmother and the *ton*.'

And there it was again, the warmth he had lived without for so long, and he wanted it for Juno if he could not have it for himself. 'I did nothing to make her feel she had a right to confide in me.'

'Most people think a child is best in the care of a woman, so I cannot see why you insist on blaming yourself for an honest mistake.'

'You do not think women must be better with children than men, then?'

She shrugged and looked uncomfortable and he reminded himself she and Turner had not had children, so that could well be a sore spot in her life. 'Some men are every bit as caring and loving as women and some females simply do not have the heart to put the welfare of a child before their own,' she answered carefully and set him wondering if her mother was as cold and selfish as his had been. If so, someone had done a fine job raising her and her brother since they were far more open to love and life than he had ever been.

'Is that the voice of experience?' he asked because he could not help being interested in her and interest was not fascination.

'No, my mother has always wanted the best for us in her own way.'

'But her way is not your way?'

'No, our standing in the world and marrying well was never important for me. I only wanted to be with a man I loved with all my heart.'

'I can see both sides of the coin,' he said and fully expected her to hotly declare he understood nothing about true love then, but she was silent, as if she was thinking about those sides and wondering how different her life would have been if she had been more wary.

She would be right about him, though; even as a spotty youth he had not managed to fall in love with an unsuitable girl. He had been too busy missing his brother and avoiding his mother's fury because he was still alive when George was dead to have had enough feeling left for the moody ups and downs of calf love. He supposed he had been too young and alone at seventeen to do more than survive when his world had turned upside down. Being called by his brother's title, knowing so much responsibility rested on his shoulders, had frozen the young man he should have been. Alaric Defford should have been free to do foolish things like fall in love with grocer's daughters and run about town with the fastest set that would have had him. George would have eyed his pranks with tolerant amusement and tugged him out when he was drowning in River Tick.

Then his big brother would have said he must do something useful with his life as a younger son, like join the diplomatic corps or enter politics. Except by the time he had been old enough to live that life George had been dead. As Lord Stratford, Alaric could not be the wild second son because if he had been wild and irresponsible nobody would have been able to look after his thousands of acres, several lofty mansions and the legion of staff and tenants who made it all work.

'Now I am older and perhaps a little wiser I realise a parent or guardian must worry about material things,' Marianne said and they were talking about mothers. At least hers had cared enough to argue with her choice of husband.

'At twenty years old I felt I had every right to ignore them and grab happiness with both hands. But how did we get around to my unwise marriage when we were talking about Darius and Fliss's wedding only a moment ago, Lord Stratford?'

'Would you consider becoming Juno's companion when they are safely married?' he said impulsively and found he was holding his breath for her answer.

At first she looked dumbfounded, then doubtful, as if she thought her ears were deceiving her. 'I... Well, I had no idea. I do not know why you would think it a good notion,' she said and shook her head as if that was all she could manage right now.

First he had kissed her, now he was blurting out his plans for a better future for her than staying here and feeling in the way or going back to her parents' house and enduring a life she had obviously not enjoyed. How inept could one man be? 'You would only have to keep her company and Juno likes you—that is all that really matters,' he said, but she was clearly bewildered by the idea.

'We only met a week ago, my lord, and you know nothing about me.'

'I have known Miss Grantham for several years and she likes and trusts you. Even on such a short acquaintance I can tell you are painfully honest. I just want Juno to be safe and happy and stop feeling like a misfit. My mother and I did that to her, Mrs Turner. Juno needs a better life and I hope you are willing to help her build it.'

'I cannot see how having a companion who married beneath her, then spent five years travelling on the coat-tails of an army on the march could give her enough confidence to rejoin the polite world on her own terms.'

Alaric heard the defensive note in her voice and cursed the two years of grief and gossip Darius told him his sister had endured in Bath before they had come here this spring. He hated the idea of her being picked on because she was different and that was what bullies always did. They must have chipped away at her confidence and her brave marriage until she felt she must point out her unsuitability before someone did it for her.

'It does not matter if she never wants to

set foot in a ballroom again, but I do want to make her happy and the first step towards that is finding her an honest and caring companion like you, Mrs Turner.'

'There must be plenty of genteel officer's widows who would guide and help her much more surely than I can hope to,' she objected.

He suspected from the thoughtful frown into the middle distance the notion was tempting her. She had a heart as soft as butter under her brusque manner and it was better to make this about Juno instead of her having somewhere to go after her brother's wedding. 'Can you think of one?' he risked asking her.

She opened her mouth to give him a list and hesitated. 'No,' she finally admitted with a sigh.

'Then will you think about filling some of the gaping holes my stupidity has left in Juno's life?'

'You could do that if you chose, my lord. She is very ready to love you.'

'Being a lord is not all velvet and ermine and learning to walk with your nose in the air and not fall over. I have a great many duties and I cannot be with her as much as I would like, so this role is really to be her companion and friend and I believe you are the right person for it. I think you love your brother too much to stay here and resent playing second fiddle to your sister-in-law.'

'Yes, yes—I admit you are right about that much at least. I do want him and Fliss to be left in peace to live well together and I know he is worried about me going back to Bath with our parents.'

'Then why not come back to Stratford Park with Juno and help us and your family?'

'Have you talked to Darius about this? You two seem to have been confiding in one another like a pair of bosom bows.'

'This is only between you and me until and unless you say yes. I would not push you into doing something you do not want to do by underhand methods.'

'I cannot make up my mind just like that. I need time to think, then discuss this offer of employment with my brother and sister-in-law-to-be.'

'And there I was, thinking you made up

your mind about things and then told your family.'

'Then kindly give me time to do so.'

Alaric still felt like a bumbler for kissing her, then springing his wonderful idea for her future on her before she had hardly had time to catch her breath. Of course she would hesitate after that and he must let the dust settle and hope she came to the right conclusion now. Although if she was not going to be living under his roof and in his employ, perhaps... No, there was no perhaps for them. She believed in love and happy-ever-after and he most definitely did not and that was that.

Chapter Eleven

Marianne carefully avoided him for the rest of the day and one or two after that. It was not until his stone masons and carpenters began work on the chapel a couple of days later that she confronted Alaric over their mission.

'You and Yelverton were so worried about your father making the journey to the next village and back to marry him to Miss Grantham I thought they might as well be wed here instead. The chapel is only a few hundred yards away, so there is no need to worry about carriages and delays if the marriage takes place here.'

'How do you know the chapel is still consecrated?'

'Because I asked your brother and he asked the local vicar.'

'You would.'

'I did and the reverend gentleman is happy to oblige the local lord of the manor so your father can perform the ceremony.'

'Smug and managing,' she said. 'I have to admire you for it,' she added, 'although I am surprised Darius and Fliss are meekly agreeing to all your plans.'

'Apparently true love means doing almost anything for your beloved.'

'Does it indeed? I doubt it will ever do so for you, my lord.'

'So do I,' he said with a pinch of real sadness under his cynical smile. He doubted he could ever be undefended enough to love beyond reason.

'And I am far too busy supervising all the maids and handymen now flocking about the house getting in each other's way to stop here and argue with you any longer,' she informed him and marched back to her housekeeping duties.

'Avoiding me again?' Lord Stratford asked softly from behind her a week after their bewildering conversation in the garden.

Marianne was surveying the now empty

and—as clean as it could be got with mops and brooms and scrubbing brushes—grand dining room. 'How *do* you manage to creep up on people like that when you still have to walk with a stick, my lord?'

'I suppose stealth comes naturally to me and if I had not, you would have left before I could get here.'

She almost smiled—no, she nearly laughed and that was worse. 'I am a very busy woman,' she told him severely instead and wished she had managed to escape him yet again. He made her feel on edge yet almost excited when he watched her with that wary warmth in his clear blue eyes. A shiver of awareness always seemed to slip down her spine as soon as she heard his voice in the distance and made her tingle all over until she managed to find a task that demanded all her attention. She had to keep on reminding herself he only wanted her for her supposed skills as a companion and that kiss in the garden was an impulse he regretted just as much as she did. 'Was there something you wanted, my lord?' she asked.

'Common sense,' he told her.

'You know I cannot supply that.'

'No,' he said with a stern look. 'You have none to spare. You are working too hard to lay claim to any of your own, never mind giving some away.'

'There is only a fortnight to go until my brother weds Miss Grantham now and there is so much left to be done.'

'And you are doing far more of it than you need to, Mrs Turner. Please stop it before you wear yourself out and ruin the day for your family.'

'My brother and Miss Grantham deserve the best wedding they can have and I will work morning, noon and night if that is what it takes to be sure they have it.'

'Which is why I sent for as many of my people as could be squeezed in here, so you would not do it all yourself to save your brother money,' he objected and he was right, drat him. 'My servants are well-trained and work well together. All you need to do is set them going and leave them to get on with their work.'

'They still need direction,' she argued stubbornly.

'Not with you to keep them going at the relentless beat you set yourself they do not.'

'There you are then, I am doing my job.'

'And wearing them out as well as yourself and I doubt your brother has ever thought of you as an employee, Marianne.'

'You cannot call me that,' she argued. She had to do something to stop it feeling so warm and intimate in this great echoing, empty room now he was in here as well.

'Why not? There is nobody else to hear.'

'I can and you know perfectly well it is not correct.'

'Yes, ma'am.'

'And I have already told you not to address me like an elderly lady.'

'Some days there is just no pleasing you, Mrs Turner,' he said with a cynical smile.

'And if you came to badger me about your extraordinary offer that I should become Juno's companion, please remember I know nothing of the polite world and please go away again.'

He stared at the newly whitewashed walls as if he found it very hard to talk about whatever it was he was planning to tell her to persuade her she was wrong. 'I must plead, then, and tell you some family history you would probably prefer not to know,' he said at last. 'My mother is a cold woman, Mrs Turner,' he admitted stiffly. 'She loved my elder brother obsessively. I thought her love for George would transfer to his only child after my brother died, but what a mistake that was.

'The Dowager Lady Stratford informed me when I confronted her with her appalling behaviour towards Juno that she had never forgiven her for not being born a boy. George's son would have inherited his title and estates instead of me and I already knew she hated me for being alive when my brother is dead, but I was too much of a fool to see the Dowager Lady Stratford does not have another jot of love in her to spare and she despises poor little Juno for not keeping me out of George's shoes when he died. So my niece grew up with the same coldness and lack of love in her life I endured as a child and you would not want her to turn out like me, now would you?'

She could hardly say he seemed to have

turned out remarkably well, considering. 'My mother can be exasperating, but at least she has always loved us under all her fuss and fancies,' she told him instead and felt very lucky indeed.

'I did not tell you as a bid for sympathy on my account.'

'You still have it.'

'She has reason to dislike me,' he argued as if he actually believed it.

'I doubt it. If you are a madman or a murderer, you hide it well and nothing less could justify her turning against her own child. Even you must have been a helpless innocent once upon a time and cannot have done anything to deserve it.'

'I suspect just being born was enough to make her hate me.'

'Why?' she said.

He hesitated and seemed disinclined to say more and she badly wanted to know now—and not for Juno's sake. 'I should not discuss such matters with you.'

'Oh, for heaven's sake, I am a widow—not a shrinking spinster likely to faint at the very mention of childbirth or the marriage bed.'

'Very well, then. The Dowager told me when we were ranting at each other in London that she loathed the indignity of being with child even the first time, but at least she birthed a healthy boy and thought her travails must be over. My father did not agree and insisted on another boy as insurance before he would excuse her from her marital duties.'

'I cannot believe you even thought about making a marriage of convenience with such an example in front of you,' she said impulsively, then put a hand over her mouth when she realised where her tongue had taken her. 'I beg your pardon, my lord,' she took it away in order to say. If Fliss heard her she would have been hurt as the possible viscountess he had picked out to marry and he must be embarrassed by her clumsiness.

'Why should you? I cannot quite believe I did it myself now matters have fallen out so much more happily for Miss Grantham and your brother. It seemed a good idea at the time, but I have had my eyes opened to how bleak a marriage of convenience can be since then by my darling mama.'

'And you and Miss Grantham are better

people than your parents,' she said, because now they were started on frank and free conversation.

'Thank you. I am no saint, but I would never force a reluctant wife to endure me in her bed for the sake of the succession. Not all the acres in the world and a far more lordly title could be worth the misery he caused, then and now.'

She nearly laughed at him for thinking any sane female would have to *endure* him in her bed. Her inner houri would leap at the chance to have him in hers if there was even a whisper of honour in it for either of them. 'I still cannot understand a mother loving one son and rejecting the next.'

'I was not her next child or the one after that.'

'She had other children besides you and your brother, then?'

'Apparently she miscarried several times and brought a couple nearly to term before they were born dead. In the seven years between George's birth and mine a baby girl survived long enough to be christened before she died as well. Then two years before me she had a boy who lived for a month before he followed his big sister to the family mausoleum. Then nothing until she was enceinte again at last and my father was wary enough by then to leave her be until I was safely born.'

'You would think she must have been so delighted when you were delivered safely she would love you all the more. I doubt you were weak or puny since you have grown into such a tall and powerful man.'

'Why, thank you, Mrs Turner. I am flattered you have noted my rude health and sterling character.'

'You mean you are too stubborn to give in over anything without a fight, I suppose? I would have to be a fool not to have noticed that.'

'Apparently my father was as well.'

'Oh, dear, he reneged on their agreement?' she said with a sad shake of her head for the stupidity and selfishness of both his parents.

'Yes, he refused to believe I would survive after so many of his hopes were dashed before I was born. I felt sorry for the Dowager for the first time in my life when she told me that by the time I was born she hated being with child so much she just wanted me out of her body and for the pain and intrusion and indignity to cease. Imagine how she must have felt when she was expected to go through all that again and again and he never stopped wanting more children from her. I never felt more guilty about a woman's lot in life and less eager for a viscountess of my own than I was when she told me how delighted she was when my father died on the hunting field and she was free at last.'

'None of it was your fault.'

'Maybe not, but the ridiculous laws of entail and primogeniture made it the fault of Viscount Stratford with all those inherited acres and estates and more houses than one man could ever live in to pass on only to a son.'

'You sound like a Jacobin.'

'I could not support bloody revolution after the Terror in France, but hearing the true reason for the Dowager's hatred of me and through me of Juno as well made me think I must be very sure the lady I marry is happy to be a mother and I have the sense never to be obsessed with the Defford inheritance.'

The idea of him wed to a woman who would tolerate him for the sake of a family made her want to cry for some odd reason, but she fought it back and hatred for the Dowager Lady Stratford was a good antidote for tears. She would like to tell the woman exactly what she thought of her for neglecting the fine boy this fine man grew out of.

'Being the victim of her husband's obsession with male heirs did not give her any right to treat you or your niece so badly. She was the adult and you were an innocent when she decided to hate you. The wonder is that both you and Juno are good people despite her worst efforts.'

'I am flattered you think so, but I owe whatever I am to my brother. George was a good man who refused to be spoilt by her devotion to him alone. He did his best to be my stand-in father when ours died soon after I was breeched. I owe him far more than he ever got back from me as his daughter's uncle and guardian.'

'I cannot understand such limits on a mother's affections, so why do you keep on trying to, Alaric?' she said, so disgusted with the woman she forgot to call him something formal.

'Well, I hope we are done with one another for good this time. I paid her debts on the understanding I will publicly disclaim any more and she intends to live abroad now Emperor Napoleon has been ousted from his throne. Apparently she is sick of me and England and I suppose you think me harsh and bad-tempered now and will refuse my offer of employment on principle.'

'No, I have no sympathy for your mother since she obviously has far too much for herself. She meant to sell her grandchild to an old man, so why would anyone blame you for making her live on her settlements in future? At least you can make a fresh start at Stratford Park now.'

'And I hope Juno is young enough to throw off the past and grow into a woman of character.'

'I might have known everything would lead us back to that topic and I am sure you could do better than me as her companion and watchdog.'

'And I know I could not.'

'Then give me the space I asked for and I promise I will go and have the bath I have been looking forward to all afternoon and to stop harrying your poor put-upon staff, my lord. I am too weary to argue with you just at the moment.'

'I doubt you are ever weary enough for that, Marianne,' he told her grumpily and turned round and strode off into the dusky shadows of the great hall, leaving her in possession of the field.

She was not sure she wanted it at the cost of all he had forced himself to tell her in the hope she would agree to his plan. And of course she was right not to tell him she feared her own weakness as far as he was concerned. It would be one way to get him to stop persuading her with his deepest darkest secrets how much Juno needed her. But she was not sure she could endure the humiliation of him knowing how much she longed for him in her bed of a night now he was staying under Darius's roof as an honoured guest instead of a patient forced on them by circumstance.

If she accepted Alaric's offer of employment, how could she resist the urge to throw herself at him when she was living under his roof instead and might well decide her self-respect and the family honour could go to blazes as long as she could be his mistress?

And he was such an honourable idiot he would probably ask her to marry him if they gave in to this ridiculous attraction that had sprung up between them more or less at first sight. She had not been with child even once during her five years of marriage to Daniel, so she could not let Alaric wed her if they did weaken and become lovers. However he felt about the Defford succession, she could not live with herself as year after year went by without an heir to his wealth and possessions and noble name. He was too fine a man to make her his mistress and she was too much of a lady to let him marry her, so she would do better to say no and go back to Bath.

However, the thought of never seeing him again—except in the distance, perhaps, when he escorted Juno on a trip to see Fliss and

she happened to be there as well—stung her
so hard she was not sure she could bear it.
So was she in love with the man? Perilously
close to it, she decided, but not quite there
yet. Best if she did not give herself time or
chance to fall the rest of the way, then. But,
oh, how she would miss him when he went
away thinking she was so hard-hearted that
even that wrenching tale about his mother's
inhuman conduct towards him as a child
could not move her to make up the similar
gaps in poor little Juno's life until now.

Chapter Twelve

'I can see what you have been doing with yourself all morning, Marianne,' Darius informed her from his place just inside the door of the last untouched bedchamber on the main level a week on from her last tête-à-tête with Alaric.

'Indeed, most of this dust seems to be on me instead of the furniture,' she said ruefully and turned around slowly so it would not shake back on to the clean bits. 'And what are you doing upstairs in all your dirt at this time of day?'

'The same as you, I should imagine—wishing I was clean.'

'I must get this room clean and cleared then put back together as neatly as I can before I can take a bath. Mama will carp endlessly about being given a lesser bedroom than Viola's or Miss Donne's if I do not get this room done in time and neither of us want her feeling put upon and prickly on your wedding day.'

'You do not have to do it all on your own. Fliss sent me up here, dirt or no, to tell you so because she is worried about you and so am I.'

'There is no need,' she forced herself to say calmly and stared at a spider that was daring to crawl into the light now she had stopped pulling down bed curtains and the dust-laden webs of its distant ancestors.

'You are avoiding us all and I will not let you, Marianne. I thought you liked living here, but maybe I am wrong and you intend to go back to Bath with Mama and Papa after the wedding.'

'No, I am not a martyr.'

'Then if you cannot endure our company why not accept Stratford's offer of employment he tells me he has made you and stop worrying about what to do next? I hate seeing you like this, Nan. I understand that my happiness with Fliss may be reminding you of what you and Daniel had and maybe living without him feels worse than before we fell in love, but we will not make you feel like an unwanted third if you stay.'

'No, please do not think that, Darius, never think like that. I am so very happy to see that you are as loved now as you have always deserved to be. I knew you could find joy and laughter with the right woman to laugh with you and remind you what a good man you are now and again when you forget it and brood about all the things you saw and did in the war. Darius the cynic was only cover for the soft heart you protected to survive that hard life, Big Brother, and Fliss is ideal for you.'

'You saw most of it as well, Little Sister.'

'Not the killing and the conflict,' she said, knowing what it must have cost him and Daniel to set out to wound and kill their fellow men. Love for this strong and loyal and, yes, soft-hearted, brother of hers was prodding her to accept Lord Stratford's offer of employment even if she was not sure it was the right thing to do. Could Alaric become a run-of-the-mill sort of lord to her rather than the special one he was now? Or would she fall even deeper under his spell than she had already?

She sighed and realised only by doing what he wanted and living as Juno's companion was she ever going to find out. It was a risk—either hurting herself or hurting Darius and Fliss by refusing to stay here and be the widow in the way. Her brother knew how much she had hated living in Bath. He would be even more hurt if she chose to go back there instead and suspicious of her true reason why. She certainly did not want anyone else knowing about these feral longings for a man she could not have.

'Why is it always one step forward, two back with you, then, Nan?' Darius asked as if he thought that sigh was for him instead of lordly Lord Stratford.

'No,' she insisted with a shake of the head to tell him she really meant it. 'I have come a long way since you inherited Owlet Manor. But today I need to be left in peace so I can get this one last room clean and usable. It will help me weather Mama's fussing and dramatising if I make her feel that she and

Papa are important here. I robbed her of the wedding she longed for when I ran off to find Daniel and her new friends shunned me when I lived in Bath. I am such an unsatisfactory daughter to her and I know she did not defend me as fiercely as she might have done because in her heart she agrees with them, but at least we still love one another. All three of us always knew we were loved by our parents, however little we understand one another. Mama cannot see why I married Daniel when there are perfectly good curates and one or two gentlemen of leisure I could have fallen in love with if I had only tried a little harder.'

Marianne thought of Alaric's description of his cold-hearted mother and shivered. His calm acceptance of a total lack of love between them still stung her on his behalf. He could so easily have grown up hating his brother for being the favourite. Marianne sighed because it felt as if an unseen tie bound her to the viscount and it was tugging at her heart more strongly with every day that passed. Could she ignore it and do as he wanted? Of course, that decision was the real reason she was keeping the rest of the world out with the dust of ages, but Darius did not need to know and worry about her even more.

'If it makes you feel better to do this, then of course you must, Nan,' he said. 'But promise me you will stop when you get this room as perfect as you can in such a short time. The rest can wait and I do not care if Fliss and I wed in a church porch and feast in a cow byre as long as we are married. Mama can boast about my splendid wedding to Lord Netherton's niece to all her friends without them knowing the east wing is in the same sorry state Great-Uncle Hubert left it in and we have borrowed half the furniture and fittings from Miss Donne's friend Mrs Corham.'

'I want your wedding day to be wonderful so you can look back on it with a smile for the rest of your lives. If Mama is carping at me and glaring at Miss Donne all day because she feels less important than Fliss's stand-in mother, I will be miserable and on edge and Fliss will be mortified. Mama is going to be a difficult enough mother-in-law without them starting off on the wrong foot.'

'Maybe so, but the maids could do this if you let them.'

'They can help now I know exactly what needs to be done in here,' she conceded with a sigh.

'Good, perhaps it will distract them from decking out my bedchamber with every bit of finery they can find,' he said and Marianne almost laughed. The dreamy look he had been wearing so often since Miss Felicity Grantham stepped into his life one hot and sunny June day took over from brotherly concern and good riddance to it. He was thinking about his wedding night now and that was a much better idea than worrying about his sister.

'I expect Fliss will like it better with a few improvements,' she said to encourage him to see those changes with new eyes.

'I was a soldier for over a decade, sister dear. I recognise diversionary tactics when I meet them,' Darius argued nevertheless.

'Then you must know how unlikely it is I

shall sit tatting while I wait for your neighbours to call,' she countered.

'I can dream,' he said lightly, but there was sadness and frustration in his eyes all the same.

He had dreamed of making a home for both his sisters, but they were too independent minded to be Squire Yelverton's dependent sisters even if he could afford to keep them. Fliss had inherited a fortune from her godmother, but Owlet Manor and its farms had been neglected for a very long time. Even thirty thousand pounds would not last forever if Darius's sisters were here to be a drain on it. Lord Stratford's offer was a godsend she would be foolish to turn down; so that was that, she would just have to polish up her willpower and try to see as little of the man as possible in future.

'Go away and dream of your bride-to-be. I am busy,' she said brusquely.

'You promised to stop trying to make this old place perfect.'

'I did not actually promise,' she said sneakily.

'Then I shall stay here until you do,' he

said, leaning against the door jamb and ignoring her hard stare at his work shirt, covered in several sorts of dirt and maybe even worse from the smell.

'Oh, very well,' she conceded wearily because she knew he would stand there however long it took her to do as he wanted. 'After this room I will stop. There are things I must do before the wedding and I suppose I had best get on with them.'

'Promise?' he said implacably.

'Promise. Except if a crisis blows up you cannot expect me to sit on my hands and pretend it has naught to do with me.'

'If Fliss or Miss Donne cannot deal with it first,' he qualified and he was right, drat him. This was going to be Fliss's home and she had every right to take over the running of it.

'I agree,' she told Darius with a bland, blank smile to stop him finding out how desolate that felt.

'Very well, I will wash and change and, if I was a stern and managing sort of brother, I might suggest you do the same before you take your luncheon with Fliss and Miss Donne and me in the parlour.'

'Luckily you are only managing, then,' she muttered.

He grinned and left her to her spider and the empty old room. To her it was a pleasure to see a place like this coming alive again and now she had to give it up. In a way this was what she used to do on the march with Daniel—wrench comfort and cleanliness out of chaos. Whatever shelter she managed to commandeer after a long and weary march or a bloody and terrible battle was soon as clean and comfortable as she could make it. Then and now it felt like the least she could do for those she loved. And this time there was the added benefit of avoiding a man she did not want to love, but dreaded she might have to if she saw too much of him. It was high time she cut impulsive, romantic Marianne out of her life for good and became careful and realistic Mrs Turner, lady's companion.

'Was there anything worth saving?' Darius asked as he came back hastily washed and wearing clean clothes. He caught her standing exactly where he left her, staring at the pile of torn-down draperies and ancient bedding as if they fascinated her. That was where dreaming got you—absolutely nowhere.

'Were you hoping there was a suite of modern furniture under the piled-up wreckage of ages?'

'I doubt the word modern is one Great-Uncle Hubert would have recognised if it was painted across the house in letters ten feet high. What I *am* hoping for is hot tea and currant buns with my luncheon and you will have neither if you do not hurry up,' he said with a frown, as if he was getting ready to worry about her all over again.

'I will, then, since I know what a glutton for currant buns you are,' she replied and went to clean up and put on a better gown until he was safely busy again. Since Miss Donne's Bet had a light hand with a currant bun, it would be a pity to miss out on them altogether.

'Felicity looks so beautiful,' Miss Donne whispered tearfully as Reverend Yelverton said the last majestic words of the marriage service over the happy couple and they faced the world as Mr and Mrs Yelverton.

'And they are so happy I have no idea why I am crying,' Marianne agreed as she watched Fliss walk down the aisle of the tiny church on Darius's arm.

'Nor do I,' the lady said as she dabbed away at her eyes with a whisper of lawn and lace and sighed happily.

'I seem to be your escort, Mrs Turner,' Lord Stratford whispered as the best man followed Darius and Fliss out with his own wife on his arm. 'I hope I will do?'

'Of course,' she said and took his offered arm and they emerged from the little church together as local children held hoops of flowers interwoven with corn over the bride and groom like a triumphal arch. The wedding party followed the bride and groom across the fields and around to the grand front of the house rather than the back door they normally used for more everyday occasions. 'It is as well it is high summer,' Marianne said as they approached the wide open front door. 'Sunlight and warmth casts such a good light on the house.'

'Indeed,' he said as if his thoughts were elsewhere.

'And Papa was so happy to marry Darius himself,' she said with an anxious glance behind them to see if her father had exhausted himself getting here.

'Marbeck has promised to stay with Reverend Yelverton until he is ready to make the return journey and as your sister is not here yet I expect all three are sitting in the shade waiting for the fuss to die down. Your father will have plenty of time to get his breath if he can walk at his own pace.'

'And Sir Harry did not mind?' The man had brought her sister all the way here in a curricle and four as well and Marianne was not quite sure she approved, even if it was an open carriage attended by a tiger and two outriders so nobody could accuse them of impropriety. She supposed the man had exerted himself to get Viola here to see Darius and Fliss marry after some domestic crisis made it doubtful Viola could have got here in time without his help.

'Marbeck is not the yahoo some of the gossips like to believe,' Lord Stratford said as if he actually liked the raffish baronet.

'Yet I cannot help but wonder why he is

trying so hard to prove his sooty reputation false today,' she said with a frown.

'Maybe he has turned over a new leaf. He has put himself out to drive your sister here and says he will drive himself back to Gloucestershire to spend a few days with his wards, so Miss Yelverton can stay and enjoy a small holiday.'

'What a considerate employer he is,' Marianne said blandly, still not sure she liked or trusted such a handsome rake with her little sister's welfare and good name.

'Whether he usually is so or not, he needs your sister a lot more than she needs him, so it is in his interests to be kind to her when he has three wards under the age of ten to cope with alone if she leaves her post. I can barely manage to look out for one eighteen-year-old with a retiring disposition myself.'

Marianne loved her sister, though, and really did not want her to suffer the sort of insinuation and slights she faced when she came back from Spain a widow. 'Maybe I am judging him on not even a whole day's acquaintance and you are right to tell me so, but I am not inclined to be fair when my sister could be gossiped about if she does not keep Sir Harry and his bad-dog reputation firmly at arm's length.'

'Hmm, I wonder,' he replied with a pre-occupied frown as he turned to watch the Reverend Yelverton join the company at last, looking none the worse for his more direct walk past the farmyard while he continued to discuss some obscure piece of scholar-ship with his younger daughter and Sir Harry Marbeck.

Marianne tried to see them through unbi-ased eyes and frowned because, never mind fairness, Viola seemed different today. She had not seen Viola since she left Bath to be-come governess to Sir Harry's wards nearly a year ago, but her sister was more animated and less tightly in control of her thoughts and emotions than she was then. Viola even seemed to move more freely as she strolled along at her father's slow pace. And what on earth had they found to talk about so in-tently with wild Sir Harry Marbeck that they hardly seemed to notice the rest of the com-pany were even present?

'Stop worrying, Marianne. Marbeck is too

much the gentleman to take advantage of a lady employed to care for his wards and living under his roof.'

'It is not his roof,' Marianne replied absently. 'And she is not your sister.'

'Yet Miss Yelverton is clearly a lady of character and I expect she has her own share of stubborn Yelverton pride to add to it. Trust her to put him firmly in his place if he steps over the line and Marbeck will be so desperate for her to stay I am sure he will not risk it. As she used to teach at Miss Thibbett's School Miss Yelverton can pick and choose who she works for and you can trust Harry Marbeck to know it and treat her accordingly.'

'Is he a friend of yours?'

'An acquaintance merely, but I do not think he is as black as he has been painted.'

'But attractive rakes like him can cloud the most sensible lady's judgement,' Marianne objected because she did not want to be fair to the dangerously attractive young baronet.

'Indeed?' Alaric said with a glint of devilment in his eyes that contrarily made her want to laugh at his almost suggestion he might have to become a rake if she liked the idea.

Perhaps laughter was the most dangerous quality a handsome employer could offer a governess or a young lady's companion, she mused, and decided to concentrate on her sister's vulnerabilities rather than her own this afternoon. 'My sister has seen far less of the world than I have, Lord Stratford,' she said primly.

'Maybe she has just seen different bits of it, Mrs Turner,' he replied almost seriously.

'Maybe,' she replied. Did he think she was being overprotective? Perhaps she was not giving her sister enough credit for being four and twenty and a lady of character. She shot a brooding glance at Viola, Sir Harry and her father and decided even if Alaric was wrong and she was right she had no cause to interfere. Viola would see it as her big sister thinking she knew best and the fragile bond between them might break for good this time. 'And I have a wedding breakfast to supervise despite my mother's best efforts to create chaos, so kindly let me get on with my last duty as housekeeper here, my lord.'

'Heaven forbid you ever shirk one of those, Mrs Turner,' he said rather wearily and she refused to meet his eyes. Hard work had been her salvation these last few months and it was very useful to hide behind at times like this. She would miss it, she decided as she glanced around the polished and immaculate hall and the wide open doors into the drawing room and the dining hall, where tables groaned with bright glass and gleaming porcelain ready for the feast. And without Alaric's help and his servants' effort she could not have achieved even half of it.

Chapter Thirteen

'Have you decided to say yay or nay to me yet, Mrs Turner?' Alaric asked her several hours later, when the last of the guests were standing about feeling awkward and Fliss and Darius had departed in a flower-decked gig for Miss Donne's house in Broadley and a private wedding night.

Miss Donne and the family were to stay here and welcome the happy couple back in the morning, then they would spend the rest of the week here before they finally left the newlyweds in peace. And all Marianne could think of was that Lord Stratford would shortly be leaving for Broadley as well. After an overnight stop at the Royal George he would come back for Juno tomorrow, then they would travel on to his grand Wiltshire home and she might never see him again if she said no.

'I am willing to agree to a month's trial. If I do not suit you or you prove to be a tyrannical employer, we can reconsider at the end of it,' she said at last. She would be a fool not to at least give it a try, would she not?

'There will be no need,' he said confidently. 'I am sure you and Juno will enjoy one another's company so much you will hardly notice my tyranny.'

'Only time will tell,' she argued and was surprised when he shook hands on their bargain and announced it to the company. Too late to go back on her word now and of course she did not want to return to Bath or stay here and play the third in Darius and Fliss's honeymoon. Alaric was cunning to make it nigh impossible for her to go back on her word and she shot him a reproachful look over her surprised mother's head even as she smiled and agreed, yes, she was very lucky and, no, she could not have told anyone sooner than this as it was Fliss and Darius's day and they deserved to be at the centre of it.

Juno was touchingly delighted with her decision and Mrs Yelverton was torn between delight her daughter was going to work for a noble family and dislike of her having to work at all.

'Is this what you truly want, Marianne?' her father asked quietly while Alaric was doing his best to reassure her mother that Mrs Turner would be valued and respected under his roof and an elderly cousin had recently come to live at Stratford Park so her good name was safe.

'Yes, Papa, you know I prefer to be occupied and Miss Defford is a bright and interesting young woman under her diffident manner. I believe I can be useful to her and my life will not be an onerous one.'

'No, but it has been so for too long. You deserve to live among good people who appreciate your fine mind and generous heart.'

Marianne blinked back tears at the quiet understanding in the blue eyes all three of his children had inherited from him. 'Thank you, Papa. I do love you and Mama dearly, but...' She let her voice tail off as she ran out of tactful words to say why she could not go home with them and endure being a chastened widow again.

'And we love you, my Marianne, but the house in Sydney Place is not big enough for us to get away from one another and I know you were not happy there.'

'I would not have been happy anywhere after Daniel was killed.'

'Maybe not, but Bath has its drawbacks as well as advantages. It is in a fine situation and we two go on very well there, but you young people need more life and freedom than a small town house can offer.'

'You were there when I needed you,' Marianne said and it was true. Never mind the less generous of her mother's new friends, she had needed to be with her parents at the darkest time in her life so far. And now she wanted the life her father spoke of and space enough to breathe. Living at Owlet Manor these last few months had taught her to value that and maybe Alaric and Juno had taught her what she had and they did not—a loving family who would always value and look after one another despite their differences.

* * *

Marianne was glad when Sir Harry Marbeck left for Gloucestershire and Viola was free to whisper, 'Congratulations', under cover of their mother's slightly drunken ramblings on the subject of undutiful daughters and their father's gentle protests they were no such thing. 'You will be much happier with them, Marianne, and Juno is such a gentle girl you should get on very well together.'

'Darius might be hurt when he finds out I do not intend to live here and Fliss was Juno's governess for several years. She might not think we are suited.'

'She is wise enough to know the girl needs to be out in the world, not tucked away at the back of beyond with two lovebirds and as they should be man and wife in peace for a while she obviously cannot stay here.'

'And when did you become so wise about love and marriage, Viola?' Marianne asked with an intent look as if to say *Don't try and turn the subject because you know I can hang on to it like a dog with a bone.*

Oh, botheration, she was interfering and

she had promised herself not to. Just as well Alaric was not here to hear her and raise his dark brows in surprise.

'I watched you fall in love with Daniel and saw that same look in Fliss and Darius's eyes today, so I have been able to observe the difference between an agreeable sort of a companion and the love of one's life, Marianne. You will just have to trust me to know my own mind and take my own risks if the time ever comes for me to jump head first into love as my big brother and sister have done before me.'

'Sometimes you find yourself landing in a mess of briars if you leap without looking,' Marianne warned, not sure if she was referring to her own feelings for Alaric or those she thought Viola was developing for her careless employer.

'Maybe if you look hard enough there is a way around the briars without getting scratched,' Viola said, 'and you know I always look before I leap, Marianne. So please stop worrying about me.'

'I have to, I am your big sister.' Marianne read her sister's silent disagreement in her stubbornly firmed chin and the way her eyes went unreadable and chilly. 'I cannot pretend it is better not to rake up the past when it stands between us, Viola. I know how much I hurt you when I left the vicarage to marry Daniel. I felt guilty about leaving you behind almost every step of the way.'

'You still went.'

'I did,' she admitted starkly, 'and I would do it again in the same situation, but somehow I would find a way to take you with me.'

'And poor Daniel would have had the weight of the law and his commanding officer's fury to contend with as well as you demanding he marry you and never mind what Mama and Papa said,' Viola the woman reasoned.

It was almost as if Viola had made herself forget the lonely child who pushed Marianne out of the door and shut it on her as if she truly hated her for leaving. She could still hear Viola's sobs through the wood as she crept downstairs and out through the back door and into the night. And the sound of her little sister's desolate sorrow at being the only Yelverton left at home haunted her all the way to Daniel's latest posting.

Even when he finally agreed to marry her at the drumhead, since she had no intention of going away until they could wed without her parents' consent, it felt wrong to do it without her little sister playing bridesmaid as they always dreamed she would when they planned their ideal weddings as little girls. 'Forgive me?' she pleaded now as she had back then, her last words to her sister as she slipped out of their shared bedroom and stole away into the night.

'Of course, I am quite grown up now, Sister. Real love and a chance of such happiness are rare and should be grasped with both hands. I did just tell you I learnt to recognise true love when I see it, so forget about whatever I said back then—I was a spoilt brat who only thought about my own wants and needs. You did what you had to do, Marianne. Mama and Papa would never have let you wed a mere sergeant and I would have been very happy for you if Daniel had not taken you away and left me to worry about both of you as well as Darius living in the midst of so much violence and unrest.'

'I was not in any danger,' Marianne argued rather lamely but of course she had been once Daniel was posted to Portugal and then Spain. She shivered at the memory of the terrifying retreat to Corunna and the running battles even as the boats took the ragtag remains of Sir John Moore's army off the shore, then she recalled Daniel's fury when the army had tried to leave his wife behind. He had refused to let them and tears threatened now at the memory of him refusing to take no for an answer as he had marched her on board one of them and defied any man to make him leave his wife behind. There were other times they had been surprised by the enemy or just got lost in a storm and it had taken days of stubborn effort to find Daniel again.

'Don't lie to me,' Viola demanded sternly and suddenly Marianne could see what a formidable teacher she was with any pupils foolish enough to try to get the better of her. 'I am truly a grown-up now and I know you must have been scared and in peril time and time again in Portugal and Spain, whatever colourful comedies about your life on the march you sent back to make Mama and Papa feel better about you being there. You must treat me like an adult if we are to truly be sisters in spirit as well as fact once again, Marianne.'

'Very well, then, I will—anything to avoid more of your icy glares.'

'I have been working on them lately,' her sister admitted ruefully and Marianne's attention snapped back to the very grown-up problem of Sir Harry Marbeck and her sister's true feelings for the wretched man.

'You have?' she said cautiously.

'I have and do not allow that vivid imagination of yours full rein because it is Sir Harry's great-aunt who has been on the receiving end of my iciest ones lately and not Sir Harry himself. If I did not stand up to the old tartar, she would have me running around at her bidding all the time instead of looking after my charges and trying to drum a few facts into their reluctant heads.'

'She sounds like a nightmare to live with.'

'No, I like her. She adds spice to the mix.'

'You really are enjoying this position, then?'

'Yes, and imagine how it would be for me as Mama's last chick if I had stayed in Bath, Marianne. Teacher or not, I was dragged off to soirées and card parties and made to play silver loo every night of the week except Sunday when I had to go and live with them before you came back.'

'So you left me to endure it and went back to live at school with a sigh of relief, then you took this post to make doubly sure you would not have to do it again, I suppose.'

'Perhaps, but you have no idea how hard I had to fight for that post at Miss Thibbett's. If not for Papa putting his foot down for once and insisting I was allowed to leave home and accept it, I would be a Bath quiz right now.'

'No, you definitely would not,' Marianne argued. 'Not with that face and blue eyes and all that lovely blonde hair. You always were the family beauty, Viola, so do not even try to tell me you did not have dozens of offers before and probably during your teaching career.'

'And it is ridiculous of you not to accept how truly lovely you are, Marianne. Even after Daniel adored you every moment you had together, and I have no doubt told you how breathtaking you are time and time again, you still refuse to see your looks are out of the common way.'

'Because they are not—I have ordinary brownish hair and trust Mama to inform me I am too thin and look older than my years the moment she arrived here.'

'I do not think Lord Stratford agrees with her,' Viola said with a sidelong glance that dared Marianne to retaliate and mention Sir Harry Marbeck.

'Lord Stratford has beautiful manners and even his worst enemy could not accuse him of being above his company.'

'Does he now?'

'Yes, and he treats all his staff with respect and consideration.'

'I am sure he does,' Viola murmured and her eyes were full of mischief and too much understanding. It felt wonderful to be teased by her sister again, but Marianne wished Viola would choose someone else to tease her about. 'Have you ever wondered if loving so deeply once would help you cope with that passionate nature of yours even better if you ever do it again?' Viola asked almost innocently.

'There is very little chance of it as far as I can see.'

'Never say never,' Viola told her in a crisp parody of their mother in Mrs Yelverton's days as the busy wife of a country vicar.

Marianne had to laugh, as her sister intended, but there was more than a pinch of sadness under it as they went arm in arm to join a half-hearted supper left over from the wedding feast. Owlet Manor was still lovely and mellow and looked like a proper gentleman's house as it basked in the evening sun, but it felt as if the glow and energy had gone out of the place for her now Alaric was no longer here.

She would be living under his roof soon so it was impossible to put the man to the back of her mind and forget she had ever met him even if she wanted to. Impossible anyway, she realised as she moved through the knot of family and friends staying the night. This should be a completely joyful occasion. Yet she had this odd sense that something crucial was missing as soon as Lord Stratford's finely sprung carriage disappeared around the first of the bends in the road.

Chapter Fourteen

As Alaric made himself climb into the carriage he told himself he had to leave Owlet Manor and the world out of time that he felt he had been living in for nigh on a month. He had meant to bring Juno with him so they would be ready to travel back to Stratford Park in the morning, but Marianne's acceptance of his offer of employment changed all that. Juno was so delighted she persuaded him to let her stay where she was for a few more days while Mrs Turner packed and said her goodbyes to her family and they had insisted they would love to have her there. Juno and the new Mrs Yelverton were close and she had a good excuse to stay, but he did not. His presence disrupted the family gathering and Mrs Yelverton Senior was on pins all the time with a real live viscount under her son's roof and her husband was embarrassed when she assumed airs to impress him.

Alaric might have dismissed her as a social climber if he had not met her children first, but now he had learnt to look beyond surface appearances and a fussy manner he rather liked the lady under the fluster and chatter. No doubt she was interfering and had been tactless with her elder daughter, but she obviously loved her children and he could see where Marianne and Darius got their energy and determination. Given the choice between his own mother and Marianne's, he knew which one he would rescue from a burning building.

He stared out of the carriage window at the darkly green trees of late summer and the fields of ripening grain they were passing at the leisurely pace country roads dictated. His life had changed so radically since he had set out from Paris to find out what was amiss with his niece, but he was not quite sure what came next. Juno would do much better now he had found her a companion instead of a heartless grandmother to keep her company, but what about Alaric Defford?

For so many years his life had been set. He had thought he would carry on being isolated from the real world by a title and possessions until he finally bit the bullet and married for the sake of an heir and even then it would be a polite sort of marriage to a well-bred and dignified lady who would not expect grand emotions from her noble husband.

Yet Stratford Park had never felt like a true home as poor rundown Owlet Manor did even before Marianne and his staff made it shine again for the wedding. But it was his family seat and he supposed it was the place he had to go to when he thought about home. Juno was familiar with it as well, even though she had been living across the park in the Dower House for most of her young life. Thank heavens Marianne had agreed to go with them when they went back—her vital presence would scout some of the ghosts from the vast house he had lived in virtually alone since George died.

Now he had solved Juno's and Marianne's lonely dilemmas in one go he should be feeling a lot better about the future. Except he ached for so much more from Mrs Marianne

Turner than he had any right to expect from her. He reminded himself about his words to her this afternoon about a true gentleman not taking advantage of a lady in his employment. 'You have been too clever for your own good this time, Stratford,' he muttered at the late summer twilight outside the window.

There was Broadley on the horizon once again now and it was still too early for him to retire to the best bedchamber at the Royal George with nothing to do but curse himself for tying himself in knots over a female who was probably barely aware he existed as a mature and potent man. He wanted her so much he might have to take up fencing and rowing and horse racing in order to give himself something physical to exhaust himself on when she was living under his roof. Then he would only need to decide where life was going to take him without Viscount Stratford's protective armour against the world to keep it at bay and all might yet be well. Hmm, it might be, but just now he felt as if he had left everything that really mattered to him in life behind at Owlet Manor. Was he cursed to always feel lonely without it for the rest of his life?

Best not think too hard about that particular version of a wasteland and he was a patient man. He could wait for Mrs Marianne Turner to make up her mind about the man under his viscount disguise and he had forgotten about boxing when he made up his list of ways to avoid throwing himself at her in a stew of lordly passion, had he not? He would be the fittest man in England as soon as his stupid ankle was back in full working order.

Three days after the wedding Marianne waved her parents and Viola off in Lord Stratford's comfortable travelling coach. Fliss and Darius were busy pretending to help with the harvest and probably wandering about staring into each other's eyes and getting in the way instead and she was escaping her packing. Her excuse was a burning need to find a book to take with her on the journey to Stratford Park a couple of counties away in Wiltshire. So she was in Great-Uncle Hubert's study tidying a small part of it because tidying was soothing and if she happened to do some dusting while she was in here nobody could deny the room needed it.

'Ah, so there you are.'

'Yes, here I am, Lord Stratford.'

'I thought you promised your brother to stop attacking his house as if your life depended on getting it clean from top to bottom.'

'I am not cleaning. I am looking for a book.'

'Then you would seem to have come to the right place.'

'Indeed.'

'And why are you wielding a duster?'

'You would not want me importing dust into your fine carriage or your magnificent country house, now would you, my lord?'

'Admit it, you are cleaning, Mrs Turner.'

'I am sorting,' she said and that was all she was prepared to admit.

'Why?'

'I have an orderly mind.' It felt anything but orderly just now and why did he have to stand so close to her in order to talk? Although she did have to admit she had only managed to clear a small space in the piles of books stacked all around the room when Great-

Uncle Hubert had run out of bookshelves, so he had little choice but to be close to her even if his presence somehow seemed to have sucked some of the air out of this dusty old book room and she was conscious of every breath he took.

'Liar,' he accused her with so much laughter in his blue eyes she smiled back at him like an idiot.

'I am sorry,' he said at last.

'Why?'

'I am not your employer yet, but I am still supposed to be a gentleman and should not close doors behind me when there is a lady in the room.'

She felt her heartbeat thunder in her ears as the musty scent of old books and the little noises of the old house shifting on its oak bones as the sun moved around the house faded and all she could see and sense was him. 'Are you?' she murmured. 'Luckily I am not a lady.'

He stepped back as if she had bitten him. 'If anyone else said the things you say about yourself, you would loathe them,' he told her furiously.

She was glad he had to shut the door to make enough space to join her in here so nobody could hear them now. 'Best do it myself rather than wait for someone to do it for me,' she replied coolly.

'And what do you think your husband would think if he could hear you say them, Mrs Turner?'

'You have no right to bring him into it,' she told him with enough anger to hide her worry Daniel would hate the lesser version of herself she became when he died.

'Your brother seems to dread throwing you back into grief so much he does not feel he can argue when you call yourself names, but I can. I do not want to, Marianne, but you can hate me without hurting yourself. I was wrong to think I could lock my feelings away after my brother died and I cannot even start to imagine how much worse it must feel to lose the love of your life, but you can take it from me, pretending not to feel at all is not really living—it is existence and no more.'

How dare he criticise her when he had no idea how it felt to lose your true love? He had just admitted he did not and he was right.

Temper hammered in her temples, but the horrible suspicion he was right was fighting it. 'You have no right to say things even my nearest relatives dare not say,' she argued.

'Darius told me the Bath tabbies made your life a misery when you were living under your parents' roof and he was still away fighting, so no wonder he does not want to upset you.'

'Even if they had welcomed me with open arms I would still just have been stumbling around in the dark after my husband was killed. I hope Darius has stopped feeling guilty because he lived when Daniel died at his side, though, and at least he has Fliss to make him see the world as it really is now,' she said and tears threatened as she remembered that terrible time in both their lives.

'While you have nobody?' Lord Stratford said so gently she had to let his words sink in and do their damage.

'Yes,' she said and a terrible sob ripped out of her like a rusty saw. 'Now look what you have done,' she told him unsteadily and clenched her fists against the fury and heartache and beat them on the air as if it might help, but of course it did not; nothing did when she let the full force of what she had lost on that terrible night at Badajoz over-whelm her.

'Come here, you stubborn woman,' Alaric said softly and pulled her into his arms so she could beat him instead, or cry if that worked better. Brave of him and she was wrong; there was comfort to be had in the world after all. Who would have thought a viscount would have a shoulder just the right height and breadth for a tall lady to weep into and feel safe as she let the storm rage at long last?

'I will damage your fine coat,' she gasped between sobs. She did not want him to let her go, but he was sure to when he felt her tears soaking into his neat but superbly cut coun-try gentleman's clothes.

'Serve me right,' he murmured and thank goodness her stupid mob cap must have fallen off so she could feel him whisper it against her unruly hair.

And Alaric just went on holding her when she could not halt the storm of tears she had probably made worse by denying it an outlet for so long. It was such a relief to let out all the hurt and loneliness she had kept to herself in her parents' little house in Bath and even when she had come here with a brother still raw from the war. Alaric whispered the occasional word of comfort as he bent over her like a protector and she felt safe. She dare not even think the word, *lover*, but there it was in the back of her mind like a siren voice. She could almost feel her eyes going red and swollen as she tried to grab back enough self-control to remember who they were and where they were before someone came in and caught him with a weeping widow in his arms.

'I must stop this nonsense,' she murmured and tried to draw back from him.

'It is not nonsense and you have at least two years' worth of Bath gossip to get out of your system,' he told her with a wry smile when most men would hastily mumble an excuse and back away.

'They were awful and I suppose seeing Mama and Papa again has reminded me of that time and how miserable I was there,' she told him with a grimace.

'Jealousy,' he told her as if it was so obvious it needed no more explanation.

'I am all but penniless and have lost the husband I eloped with—how can anyone be jealous of me?'

'You are a beautiful woman and that is a black mark against you for the likes of them. And you have had what they never can and never will have themselves because you dared everything for love. Can you imagine a single one of them giving up their comforts and position for a man even if they loved him to distraction?'

Marianne disregarded his flattering notion she was beautiful, but she did think hard about some of her mother's cronies and the little lives they led. She almost laughed at the very idea of a single one following in the tail of an army to be with the man they loved. 'No,' she said as all the petty limits they put on their own lives suddenly struck her as pitiful and so very unimportant she wondered she had ever let them make her feel less than they were.

'Neither can I, nor a sensible man asking them to. They would make his life a misery and I suspect they bullied and belittled you because you made their lives look so small and dull in comparison.'

Tears had made her eyes sore and the occasional sob still shook her, but he had not pulled away in disgust. Alaric's strength and humanity seemed to have melted something icy and painful inside her and she was glad. She felt as if she could breathe more freely without it, even if every breath she took drew in his warmth and the pure temptation of being alone with him in a musty old room. Reminding herself she must look terrible, she scrubbed at her eyes with her handkerchief. 'How did you know all that?' she asked him huskily.

'Perhaps I know you and all I need to do is imagine the small lives they lead and contrast them with you and there you are—jealousy and guilt. It is obvious. No wonder they disliked you, Marianne. How dare you be twice the woman they are?'

'A few were men,' she qualified with a shudder.

He frowned. 'Damn them for being spiteful when you rebuffed them, then.'

'How did you know they tried to seduce me first?'

'I have eyes and a heart and feelings, Marianne,' he told her as if he thought she might not have noticed.

'I know,' she said soothingly, but it seemed to make him even more gruff and grumpy.

She made the mistake of patting his shoulder to soothe whatever ailed him and felt the fine tension in his body. Intent on what she wanted for once she stood on tiptoe and kissed him, quick and hard, on the lips. She would have swiftly backed away if he had not taken over as if he was starving for her, then deepened it into something more intense. Their kiss in the garden had felt warm and wonderful, but this was far more passionate, much more demanding.

She felt little pulses of lightning shimmer through her wherever he touched her, but sanity might have saved them if she had not felt hesitation in his touch, as if he was afraid he might hurt her. She murmured a wordless argument and gasped at the need blazing inside her when she opened her mouth against his and forgot all about lords and soldier's widows in the glorious heat of the moment.

Passion hot and heady flamed between them. This time her tongue was bold and teased his firm mouth, then tangled with his. She ran a shaking hand over his crisp dark curls and loved the freedom of being able to touch him. She explored the nape of his neck with a touch of wonder at his latent strength under her fingertips. He was so different from Daniel she felt like a traitor for a moment as she thought about then and now, but the richness of the moment soon swallowed it up. Alaric was always himself, just as Daniel had been, and right now he was a novel pleasure under her exploring hands, then her mouth again once they took in enough air to risk driving one another out of control.

His hands were broad and strong on her back and she wriggled closer and gazed into his eyes for a luxurious moment. He stared back at her with his blue eyes blazing emotion she was desperate to read, but could not quite decipher. She wondered why his eyes were much the same colour as her own, but so very different. His pupils flared with what looked like strong, almost desperate feelings.

'Marianne,' he breathed her name so huskily it sounded like a magical spell. What they both wanted was clear enough from the grinding need inside her, but from the regret in his eyes he was not going to allow them to have it. Now his touch was meant to soothe instead of inflame. The loneliness of him drawing away from her made her want to cry, again, if she had any tears left. Except she felt them prickle her sore eyes for him this time, for the loss and lack of him even when he was still warm and strong and very much alive against her wanting body.

She shook her head. 'Alaric,' she whispered in the book-stale air of Hubert Peacey's private lair. 'You stopped,' she half accused him, although anyone might have come in and caught them entwined like lovers and that really would not do.

'I had to,' he said on a long sigh of what sounded like regret. 'Anyone could have come in and found us locked in each other's arms,' he echoed her thoughts huskily.

'I suppose that would have hurt your pride and your reputation.'

'It is not me I am worrying about,' he argued impatiently.

'Do not concern yourself about me, my lord. I will survive. I am quite good at it by now,' she said flippantly and saw fury blaze in his eyes this time.

'Survival is not good enough for you, or me. We have both survived for long enough and there has to be more than that from now on.'

'Yes, there must be to make it worthwhile,' she agreed, but it was all she could offer right now.

They avoided one another's eyes as the afternoon sun suddenly crept out from behind the clouds outside and edged curiously in around the blinds that had frayed and faded and no longer protected Great-Uncle Hubert's precious books as well as they should. That sun was already lower in the sky and soon it would be autumn and they would both be in Wiltshire at famously grand, classically splendid Stratford Park. And he would be my lord there and she would be an upper servant.

Marianne the lover screamed at the rest of her to seize what she could, while she could have it. 'I am probably barren, Alaric,' she told him painfully and who asked the houri to speak?

'And I probably do not care,' he said, but how could he not?

He was a lord as well as master of large estates and all the family history dragging behind him like a ball and chain.

Ah, of course—he could not marry her, could he?

Not only was she the widow of an enlisted man and a mere vicar's daughter, but she could not give him the children he needed so badly. A mistress who was unable to breed a pack of little bastards to complicate matters when he took a wife and bred his heirs would save him so much complication.

'Well, I do,' she said. She straightened her wilting stance, telling herself not to feel the loss of those children, bastards or no. She longed for them so desperately even as she eyed him militantly and hurt herself on a shattered dream she had not even known she had until now. Now she would have to regret not carrying his child as well as her abiding sorrow that she had never borne Daniel one either. Suddenly that felt like agony and something feral uncurled inside her to defend her from any more of that.

'And you intend to use it as yet another weapon to keep me at a distance, I suppose?' he said as if *she* was hurting *him* instead of the other way around and for no good reason either.

'No, it is the plain truth, so I do not need a weapon to fight off amorous noblemen,' she snapped, her past pain and frustration at her childlessness driving her into a fury way beyond any offence he might have offered her if she gave him a chance to. 'And I would not marry you even if you wanted me to. Now if that is all I really must wish you good day, my lord. I am a very busy person and if you still want me to pack up my life once again and come with you to Stratford Park I need to hurry now, or is that scheme all over after this whatever it was we just did together?'

'Of course I want you to come with us and you agreed to become Juno's companion for at least a month, so do not use this.' He stopped and looked helpless and driven and even a little bit hurt for a moment before he stamped Lord Stratford back on his face and manner and his gaze went stony.

He even imposed rigid control on his sensitive mouth and that was what made her stop and think because his mouth was so warm, provocative, so intimate and right on hers only a few seconds ago and now she was treating him as an enemy. Brought up short by his withdrawal of all warmth from her, she realised where her stupid temper and frustrated maternal instincts had taken her and was ashamed.

She had invented most of this painful scene by deciding his motives and intentions towards her without knowing what they really were. Temper put up a wall between them and she had no idea how to tear it down again. Her fury at an improper offer he had never even begun to make had led her to break something precious. Alaric looked so hurt before he shut her out that she felt more alone than she ever had before as they stood so close and so distant in this musty old book room and listened to one another breathe.

'This altercation,' he went on stonily as if that was all it had ever been and never mind the odd kiss or two, 'of ours cannot be allowed to disappoint Juno so deeply when we have both promised to try and make her a better future.'

'I will not renege,' she said with a little bit too much dignity as well. This was her fault, she decided as she stared down at the one small pile of books she had managed to rescue from the dusty chaos all around them. Her insecurities were too ready to come to the fore and prod her into a defensive temper. Because she was so afraid she felt too much for him, she walked on briars when they were together, as if that was all she deserved.

This time she was stiff and defensive and far too sensitive to hurts he probably never meant her to feel and what a hopeless pair they were. It was probably just as well she had scuppered any chance he might be stubborn and reckless enough to ask her to marry him, whatever it was he felt for her. She wondered if either of them were quite sure what that was and bit back a regretful sigh.

'I will have to hurry up if I am to be ready

to leave tomorrow,' she said as she looked down at that pile of books as if she was fascinated when she could not have said what they were or who wrote them if her life depended on it.

'I shall not inflict myself on you once you are living under my roof,' he said.

'I kissed you,' she argued stiffly.

'Whatever we did, I should not have let it happen.'

'We kissed one another because we could not help it and now we can, so that should not be a problem for us any more, should it?' Suddenly she wanted to go with him so badly the idea of staying here looked faded and blank. Was there ever a more contrary female than Marianne Turner, née Yelverton? she asked herself as she traced the tooled leather cover of one of Great-Uncle Hubert's most prized volumes and still had no idea what it said.

'Will you come to Stratford Park with us and keep your word to Juno, then?'

'Stop making everything in your life about her, Alaric,' she told him earnestly, because at least she could argue with his overdeveloped sense of guilt even if she could not take back what she had said and make this distance between them vanish. 'Juno is too young and confused to take the weight of your guilt on her shoulders. You told me to stop being ruled by the past and start living again so I will if you will.'

'Maybe I lack your courage.'

She shook her head and refused to meet his not-quite-as-chilly look. 'No, I am a coward,' she said sadly and opened the door and made herself walk away from him. She felt his gaze on her back and still made herself keep doing it. She did not want to carry the image of Alaric staring after her as she went all the way up the stairs and branched off to her room at the front of the house a floor further up in the attics because she told herself she had always liked the view and nobody else ever came up here. Except of course a picture of him before she managed to turn her back and leave did stay with her and she could not see the mellow afternoon countryside for the blur of yet more tears she blinked back furiously.

He looked so bleak and alone against the

world again and it was lonely and stark up here as well, view or not. So much of her wanted to run back downstairs to tell him he could have anything he wanted of her; she would do for him what she had for Daniel and risk everything for love. Except this time she would have to cast every last caution to the four winds if she truly loved him. If she did that, she could not shackle him to a barren woman even if she insisted love was enough and would she have the courage to face the world as Viscount Stratford's mistress and not his wife?

It would be even more of a transgression than loving Daniel seemed to the wider world, but she had never regretted that one so maybe it would not be as empty and echoing as the word 'mistress' looked from outside. Yet what if he discovered love was not enough? What if he looked at her in five years or ten or even twenty and realised he had sacrificed too much for her? No, it felt like a cutting off of something precious and potentially wonderful, but maybe that petty, stupid quarrel she had forced on him was for the best.

'Forget he is anything more than your employer from now on, Marianne,' she whispered to herself once she was safely inside her bedroom with her back pressed against the door as if to keep wild and sensual Marianne out. Of course he had not come up here looking for her; Lord Stratford was too honourable to pursue a woman who had said no to him. 'And stop lying to yourself,' she told herself disgustedly. 'You did not say no, he did when he called a halt to that kiss. You would have gone on saying yes until anything else was a technicality.'

Just as well he had, then, since she could not endure being cut off from her brother and Fliss and Viola for the sake of a scandalous liaison with a man so far above her touch. She did not have a thick enough skin to be anyone's mistress, even if she could face the idea of never seeing her family again as the price for the sensual pleasure she knew she would experience in his bed. And what would Papa think when he found out his elder daughter had become a scarlet woman? He would be heartbroken and that was that, then—the last nail in the coffin of Marianne the mistress.

It did not stop her aching for Alaric the man while she got ready to pack her life up again. At least he was in Broadley by now, not a floor down and a few sturdy planks of oak away from her as he had been for the last few weeks. Even that was not nearly far enough away to let her rest peacefully tonight and somehow she had to learn to stop being a fool about a man she could not have.

Chapter Fifteen

After years of holding himself aloof from strong emotions, Alaric felt so many tearing away at him now it was as if he was making up for a drought. She was so vulnerable, the real Marianne under Mrs Turner's brisk efficiency, and it was too soon to risk everything they could be before he knew it was for good. What a fine pair they were; him guarding his heart after losing George and succeeding to a title and estates he never wanted and her hiding so much hurt and grief for her Daniel behind relentless hard work.

This afternoon she had trusted him enough to cry in his arms and let some of it out and that had made him feel proud and racked with guilt at the same time. He had wanted her so much even while she wept for another man against his shoulder as if her heart might break. No wonder she had responded when he kissed her so lustily; she was overwrought, all her emotions too close to the surface, and she had trusted him. Then she had distrusted him and then she went sad and distant and mysterious on him and he would never understand women as long as he lived.

'Brute,' he still accused himself as he rode back to Broadley.

He had recognised something exceptional and significant about Marianne the moment they met and now he felt a fool for not realising how much she meant to him until they quarrelled and he did not know how to cross the barriers they had each put up to keep the other at a distance again. He had known she was true and strong at first sight, despite the snap of temper in her fine eyes and her impatience with lords like him. So, yes, Marianne tugged at his senses and challenged him and made him someone better than he was before he met her. And he wanted to confront her with everything they could be to one another if they only dared, but caution whispered it was too soon. And how could he reveal his dreams and dilemmas to her now he had persuaded her to become Juno's companion? He had done it to give her a place to go when her brother married, but doing it left him tied hand and foot.

How could he tell her he felt explosive and on fire and desperate for her in every inch of his body and all his wildest fantasies when she was still grieving for her husband? Even if she was not in his employment and would not soon be living under his roof, how could he tell her that? Well, she had said they should give each other a month's trial, had she not? Best hold her to that limit and maybe, after a month of trying his hardest to be a good and unthreatening viscount, he could finally manage to convince her he was a better man than the evidence so far suggested.

'Juno? Juno? Where are you? The carriage is coming down the drive and your uncle is here to escort us on the first leg of our journey to Wiltshire.'

Marianne realised at breakfast this morning that the girl had grown more silent as the day to leave Owlet Manor came closer and she had barely managed to eat a thing today now it was actually here. Marianne urged Fliss and Darius to say their goodbyes, then go on a visit to Miss Donne so there would not be quite so much of a break when the time came for Juno to leave. Now Seth and Joe were carrying their luggage for the journey out for the grooms to buckle or tie in place and the rest had gone ahead by carrier. Lord Stratford was waiting outside on a fine horse obviously much more suited for a gentleman to ride and waiting to escort them to his home and Juno was nowhere to be seen. Marianne heard her own voice echo up into the lofty roof timbers and beside that there were only a few murmurs as the coachman and grooms got on with preparing the luxurious carriage for the journey. She shouted Juno's name again; silence met her voice again and felt like far too much of it for comfort as her heart began to race. That terrible feeling of urgency she remembered when Juno was missing felt like ice as a fear that history was repeating itself shivered down her backbone. She ran up the stairs as fast as she could raise her skirts and sprint.

'Juno?' she shouted again as she pelted

down the bedroom corridor and heard only the sound of her own feet thumping on ancient oak floorboards and the echoes of her own voice again. 'Juno?' she repeated, desperate now as she ran into the room expecting to find it empty and Juno halfway to goodness knew where. She was so convinced she was right that she nearly turned away too soon and missed the glimpse of skirts and petticoats that was all she could see of Juno from the doorway. She peered around it and saw the girl sitting on the floor in the furthest corner of the room, rocking herself backwards and forwards like a desolate child. 'Oh, Juno, why are you down there? Whatever is the matter?'

'I cannot, I just cannot,' Juno wailed incoherently and Marianne almost wished her own mother was here, or Viola. Or anyone who had experience of sobbing and incoherent girls who were not yet quite old enough to really be women would do right now. 'Tell Uncle Alaric I am sorry,' the girl said.

'You must tell him that yourself,' Marianne said and there was her lifeline. He was Juno's guardian and protector; he would know what to do and say. Or if he did not he would just have to learn fast.

'Lord Stratford!' She ran back down to the head of the stairs, calling out his name. 'Tell Lord Stratford he must come inside and you had best have the horses unharnessed and taken off to the stables, Joe. There has been a slight delay to our plans.'

Now she was feeling guilty at her panic about having to deal with Juno's distraught tears and that strange frozen look on her poor woebegone face. Alaric dashed in through the front door, then took the stairs in as few bounds as he could and she was so glad of him she almost wept herself.

'What is it?' he demanded curtly.

'I have no idea, but Juno needs you,' she told him breathlessly and was almost on his heels when he had to grab the upright of the door to stop himself in his headlong haste to get to his niece. Then he was sitting down by Juno on the floor and doing what Marianne ought to have when she found her there. He simply pulled her into his arms and rocked her like a little child as she howled into his superfine coat.

The poor man would be getting through them by the dozen if distraught females kept on weeping all over him like this, Marianne mused, feeling decidedly surplus to requirements, yet still she could not make herself go away and leave them in peace to talk about whatever Juno wanted to talk about.

Juno surprised Marianne after a few moments of unrestrained woe by sitting upright and fighting back her tears. She owed the girl an apology for expecting her to go on sobbing until she was so incoherent with misery she had to be put to bed. 'I thought I could, but I cannot,' she said rather bravely. 'Stratford Park,' she explained as a sob and a shiver hit at the same time and she buried her head in Alaric's shoulder again and seemed to find some of his strength in there. She shook her head as if she was furious with herself for reacting in this way.

'I have heard of it,' Alaric said lightly and Juno actually managed a laugh.

'The girls from London, I simply cannot go back and face them, Uncle Alaric. I tried so hard to find the nerve to, but I truly cannot do it.'

'Ah, and now we are getting to the heart of things at last. Why did you not tell me about them before I set all these ridiculous plans in motion, love?'

'I wanted you to be proud of me. I want to be brave and strong and look them in the eye and show them I am not a looby or a wantwit or even a silly little wallflower. I am, though, because I cannot do it.'

'Is that what they said? And who are they?'

At last it all came tumbling out—the full story of Juno's miserable debut Season in so-called polite society. Never had Marianne been more grateful she was too humbly born and Papa too poor for her to do more than attend a few local parties and a subscription ball at the Assembly Rooms in the nearest town when she was old enough to be considered officially out.

'I cannot understand why those girls turned against you,' Marianne said from her place on the bed where she had sunk while she heard all the vicious tricks a few haughty young women had played on Juno once they discovered they could get away with it, 'especially when some of them are your uncle's neighbours and should have known better.'

'At first they were eager for me to join in with them, but I suppose I am too quiet and I had never been to the waltzing parties or any of the events their mamas arranged for them before they were officially out so they were at ease and I was not.'

'Idiot, I should have thought of that,' Alaric chided himself.

'No, Grandmama should. She took your money and spent it lavishly on parties and grand toilettes for herself and entertaining her friends, like that horrid man she was so insistent I had to marry. She should have done all the things for me other girls' relatives did. I will not have you blaming yourself for her selfishness, Uncle Alaric,' she told him rather sternly and Marianne was very tempted to nod her agreement.

'Whatever I can or cannot blame myself for, we clearly cannot go to Stratford Park today, Jojo. If you will unpack one of those boxes the men have been so busy strapping safely to my travelling carriage so you may wash your face and brush your hair and meet me downstairs when you are ready, we three can decide what to do next. Come, Mrs Turner, I believe Juno will come about if we leave her in peace for a few minutes to compose herself.'

Marianne followed him out like a faithful sheepdog after her shepherd and expected to be dismissed from a position she had told herself she did not want very much anyway. Now it was fading away it seemed like a lost opportunity to be close to the man without anybody realising how badly she wanted to be close to him and that was a giveaway of her true feelings, was it not? She obviously felt far more for Viscount Stratford than she had ever wanted to feel for another man after Daniel died and this time it could not go anywhere at all. Just as well if he did dismiss her, then.

'I should have known,' she said as soon as they were out of Juno's hearing.

'Nonsense, and if we are both going to blame ourselves nothing will get done. We simply need to find another place for her to go since I do not have the heart to force her to face those little harpies. If you will help me to do so, I will be grateful and I am sure Juno will be as well.'

'You do not mind that your plans are spoilt?'

'No, I do not like Stratford Park very much myself so I will not be heartbroken if Juno does not want to live there.'

'But isn't it very grand indeed?' Marianne said, the radical idea a man might not actually like his ancestral home making him seem less lordly and more human. Sometimes she really wished he was hard-hearted and arrogant so he would seem less appealing to a susceptible idiot like her.

'It is, very grand. I am not very fond of grand—I have discovered lately that I much prefer comfortable. If your brother would only sell it to me, I would far rather live here than in a vast Palladian folly like Stratford Park.'

'He will never do that, he loves it here.'

'I know, pity,' he said with a grin as if he really was relieved not to be going back to huge and famous Stratford Park.

'What do you think you might do instead?'

'If you and Juno are agreeable, we could

travel until the roads become too difficult to do so freely, then we can think again. It might be good for Juno to wander about her own country and explore whatever bits of it take her fancy at the time.'

'But you are an important man of affairs and I know you have obligations to your tenants and neighbours. At least Darius only has three farms to worry himself over and all of them are within easy riding distance.'

'I envy him more and more every day,' he said lightly and Marianne almost believed him.

After a day to regroup and for Juno to recover from her tears and chagrin, they ended up taking a very leisurely journey up into Shropshire for a week or more. Then they explored Cheshire for another week or two. Derbyshire came next and by then it was agreed that Lord Stratford would soon have to leave them to their travels while he attended to some of that business he and Marianne had talked about at Owlet Manor and he also met his agent and did all the things conscientious viscounts had to do.

Marianne and Juno shared a maid now and the girl sat silent and rather glum on the seat opposite them as they rolled down yet another country road to a country town where they were to spend another countrified night. The girl could not be much older than Juno, but she ghosted about their bedchambers night and morning, laying out this and that and being so silently helpful Marianne felt inhibited by the barriers between servants and served for the first time in her life.

The maids at the vicarage where she grew up had been cheerfully loud, tossing remarks back and forth to one another as they cleaned or cooked or helped the children with their dressing and undressing until they were considered old enough to do it themselves. This sort of service was different and Marianne had to find the line superior servants seemed to want to hold between them and their noble employers and even with Miss Defford's companion. She felt subtly put in her place by the silent efficiency of the girl and even the grooms and coachman said very little as they sped through the sleepy countryside. Lord Stratford rode ahead most of the time, but he was often wrapped up in his own thoughts even when they came together at those inns along the way where they were fussed over and spoilt because of his rank and power. Perhaps he was simply enjoying the peace and quiet and the changing scene. He was obviously completely fit and healthy again after his accident, so maybe he was enjoying travelling about his homeland after several months spent among the tension and furore of a Paris struggling to come to terms with the downfall of their beloved Emperor.

Marianne sighed and shifted in her comfortable seat and heartily wished she was not such a fool. All three of them were embarking on a new life, even if this current one did feel a bit like a limbo between their old and new ones. Lord Stratford had sent in his resignation to the government, so he told Juno there would be no more duties distracting him from his family and estates from now on. Whatever he had done for them in the past, he must be a reliable and subtle diplomat if the men of power relied on his tact and discretion to smooth out some of the bumps in the Duke of Wellington's rocky road as British Ambassador to France.

Marianne knew from experience how abrasive and pernickety and downright rude the great man could be, even if he was also steadfast and subtle and brave and almost a genius when it came to the delicate balancing of troops and terrain in battle. She admired the Duke deeply and even the sight of him steady and unquestionably in charge would put heart into his army. His men had trusted him not to waste their lives on vainglory, but they did not adore him as so many Frenchmen almost seemed to worship Napoleon Bonaparte.

The carriage rounded a long bend and now she could see Lord Stratford riding in front of them again. Would this journey be less tedious if he chose to join them in the carriage rather than ride ahead in solitary state? He seemed so at home in the saddle she supposed he enjoyed the exercise and it was a little stuffy in here so who could blame him for avoiding it? However well-sprung and well-cushioned a carriage was, the novelty of travelling in such style soon wore off as mile after mile sped past and heat began to build as the sun came out. She tried not to let her gaze linger on Lord Stratford's lithe form to distract her from this jolting box on wheels. They could not even open the windows more than a crack for the pall of dust the horses were kicking up.

Alaric sat his powerful grey as if he had been born in the saddle and what was he going to do with himself now he had laid aside his self-imposed duties? The man she had begun to know under the haughty aristocrat was too restless and clever to be content with the life of a country squire for very long. She frowned at his strong back, powerfully muscled shoulders and narrow flanks and wished he was less compellingly masculine. The idea of him as an idle viscount bent on pleasure seemed laughable right now, but would he be restless and bored after a few weeks of country life and be tempted away to London for the Little Season?

She felt the hum of excitement under this odd new life she was going to be living stumble and halt at the thought of him not being with them and caught herself out in a lie. It was not entirely for Juno's sake she had agreed to this wandering journey. Of course she had nowhere she wanted to go after Darius and Fliss married and the alternative was finding work with strangers, if they would employ her, or going back to live with her parents in Bath. But there was a thread of fantasy and need under all the good reasons she had given herself to be here. She wanted him to look at her with sharp interest and seductive intent again just as he did in Great-Uncle Hubert's study that memorable day. And she did not want her own stupid insecurities to spoil it this time. Yet why would he risk such a stinging rebuke for things he had never said again? He would not, of course he would not, and he must be uncomfortable at the very thought of that frustrating encounter. So every day she told herself there would be something so fascinating and breathtaking to see out of the carriage window she would forget to watch for him like a fool and wish those hasty, bad-tempered words unsaid. And every day she was disappointed.

'We will soon be in Buxton, Mrs Turner,' Juno said as if she thought Marianne was flagging and needed encouragement.

'When will you remember to call me Marianne, Juno?' Marianne said and tore her gaze from Lord Stratford's lithe but powerful form to meet Juno's eyes.

'What if I forget and do so in public?'

'It does not matter since I hope we are friends and we can be those in public as well as in private and you really need to stop worrying about what other people will think of you all the time.'

'That is what Uncle Alaric says, but I cannot bring myself to be bold and brave and I fear I shall never be a credit to him.'

'You already are and he loves you as you are, Juno. Do you think that will change if you say a wrong word or speak out of turn by accident? If you do, then I do not think you understand him at all.'

'Perhaps not, but you obviously do,' Juno said and there was the intelligence and underlying strength of character Alaric was intent on bringing to the surface more of the time, although Marianne preferred it when Juno was not using them on her.

And this silly preoccupation with Lord Stratford had to stop. She would remember to call him that even in her head from now on; Alaric would not do for a lord and his niece's paid companion. Marianne shifted and shot a wary glance at the maid, but the girl had succumbed to the warmth of the day, the rocking of the coach and the sheer boredom of trailing around the country on the whims of the aristocracy and was fast asleep again. The girl must have slept her way through half of her native land by now.

'It does not take a great deal of insight to see love behind His Lordship's iron determination to find you when he got to Broadley so travel stained and exhausted you would barely have recognised him. A shame, perhaps, that he was shaven and tidied up by the time you saw him that day; if you had met him weary and desperate for news of you as I did when he rode in soon after the dawn you would know how deeply he longed to find you safe and well and how much he loves you.'

'And I might not have made him go away and he would not have been thrown from that horrid horse and given us all such a terrible fright.'

'We would probably not be sitting here having this conversation then, since His Lordship and I did not like one another very much at the time. I dare say he would never have realised my sterling qualities and companionable virtues for the bad blood between us back then and, if you had agreed to go back to Wiltshire with him, I would never have got to know you better either and I would miss you, Juno.'

'No, you would not, because you would never have found out how wonderful and unique I am and what excellent company I can be, but I am very glad we did stay at Owlet Manor and that you are my companion now.'

'Thank you, so am I,' Marianne said, but she was not quite sure she really meant it. If Lord Stratford had only gone away again as soon as he reclaimed his niece, maybe Marianne would have forgotten about him by now. At least then her heart would not ache whenever she thought how differently matters might have fallen out if he was born a humbler man and she was a more confident woman.

Chapter Sixteen

After Lord Stratford went off to be a dutiful lord and look after his grand house and estates and vast numbers of tenants' interests for a while it felt lonely and a little bit pointless and meandering to keep on travelling without him. Marianne sat in a coffee room of yet another comfortable inn one morning, brooding about whether it was more painful to see him every day and not be able to touch or be touched by him or not to see him at all and miss even the sight of him. Sometimes it felt as if half of her was always somewhere else, wondering how he was and what he was doing and if he missed her, too. Probably not, she concluded and sighed over her letter from Darius and Fliss and almost wished she was back at Owlet Manor with them, except Alaric would not be there either.

'You look very pensive, Marianne,' Juno interrupted her reverie and made her start guiltily.

'I was daydreaming,' she replied truthfully.

'About sad things from the look of you,' Juno said gently. 'Did you love your husband so very much?' she asked impulsively, then looked cross with herself for asking. 'I do beg your pardon. Of course you do not want to talk about him to a stranger. How clumsy of me.'

'No, it was not and you are not a stranger.'

'I know I am young and must respect your privacy as Uncle Alaric told me to, but I cannot help wondering how it feels to be in love. How do you know when you have found your special he, that he is not just another gentleman with a pleasing face and form and gentle enough manners?'

'Of course you must ask such questions or how are you to learn more about the world? Yes, I did love my husband, very deeply. I miss him so much at times it feels as if I only lost him yesterday and at others he seems so far away from me I think I must have imagined so much about him I know to be true. I dare say none of that makes any sense to you, but I pray you will never have to find out for yourself how it feels to love someone deeply and sincerely and then lose him, Juno. I hope your love affair turns out to be a lifelong one when you finally get around to falling in love with a man who deserves you.'

'But how will I know it is really love I am feeling? How did you know your husband was going to be the one you would love for life when you met him?'

'I—' Marianne broke off and met Juno's painfully honest blue gaze and for a moment she could not get past the fact her eyes were so much like her uncle's the resemblance jarred her heart with pain and nostalgia and made her think too hard about love again.

Now she was missing Lord Stratford instead of Daniel Turner and it felt disloyal. She suddenly had a mental picture of her beloved husband turning around to smile one of his loving, glowing smiles at her as he walked away with a wave towards another path she had to take without him now. This time the tears could not be held back.

She had been wrong at Owlet Manor when

she cried all over Alaric—she was a watering pot. The panic and remorse in poor Juno's face at the sight of her tears made her reach for her sensible handkerchief and scrub them away. The poor girl obviously thought she had caused these tears, but they were Alaric's fault and she could not even be furious with him to stop it hurting. Under all that lordly temper and arrogance he was a good man and would probably hate the idea of causing her pain, so Juno must never find out she sometimes cried over him and not just Daniel.

She wondered as she stared out of the coffee-room window to try and fight her eyes dry if it would truly be better if she had never met the man. No, she would have missed so much. She shook her head at the thought of the hollow that she would have left in her life. He had marched into it and forced her bruised emotions back to life; it was much better to feel than simply exist from day to day, so she had to be glad of him. She sighed for the simple inevitability of her and Daniel's love for one another and supposed they were much luckier in love than Lord Stratford and Mrs Turner were fated to be. So where were they before she diverted herself with a new set of tears? Ah, yes, love. At least she could talk about her feelings for Daniel openly.

'I was not the noble heroine you seem to want to paint me as when I first met my husband, Juno. I could not believe I could really be in love with my brother's sergeant and fought my feelings for him for as long as I could fool myself it was simply not possible,' she said as honestly as she could with that forbidden *and this time I shall have to fight them for the rest of my life* caveat in her head. 'Daniel was Darius's steadfast comrade in arms and saved his life more than once and I clung to all the distinctions of rank and fortune between us for a while, as if I was a princess and he was a peasant. I wonder he did not simply shrug and march away from me with barely a second thought.'

'Obviously you did not cling to them all that hard,' Juno argued.

Marianne decided she would have to be careful not to make it sound a wildly romantic tale and tempt Juno to follow her example. There could never be two men like Daniel even if there were any more wars to fight and God send there were not. 'I had enough of my mother in me back then to do my very best to deny the fire and warmth that sparked between Daniel and me from the first moment we laid eyes on one another, Juno,' she continued as carefully as she could with the memory of that time to warm her with a smile for the man who had marched into her heart and stolen it without even trying. 'His honesty and big heart and the uniquely lovable fact of him wore my snobbery down in the end. I knew I could never even think about being happy with another man while he was alive somewhere to let me know I was wrong to even try to forget him inside a more suitable marriage for a vicar's elder daughter.'

And apparently I still possess that genius for falling in love with unsuitable men.

Marianne finally admitted the truth to herself. She was no happier about this admission of her true feelings for a man than she had been seven years ago when she finally accepted the fact Daniel would always hold her heart, never mind him being a suitable life partner or being able to keep her and any children they might have in the sort of comfort, if not much luxury, she was used to as a lady of gentle birth.

'I should never have asked you to talk about this when it obviously upsets you. Please will you ignore my nosiness, I truly did not mean to make you cry.'

Impossible to say it was the awful realisation she was actually in love with Juno's uncle that did that, not only the memory of Daniel being so gruffly silent for once when they first met and so gallantly determined not to act upon the unseemly spark of attraction between himself and Lieutenant Yelverton's sister. 'Sometimes we have to cry, Juno. It is the only right response to a situation we have no control over. I learned to hold my tears in and pretend not to be feeling anything very much while I lived with my parents in Bath after Daniel died and grief twisted in on me until I felt dead inside. Anything is better than living in a world that suddenly feels grey and hopeless and I hope I never have to go back to the wretched place again and relive the sorrow I lived with there. If you have a yearning to see the place, I would be grateful if you would dismiss me and engage another companion because I cannot endure it.'

'That I do not and even if I did I would rather have you and put off a need to visit a place that sounds far too full of dull people without enough to do. And I do hope I will be considered a disgrace to my family and far too disreputable to be allowed to join the gossips in Bath if I never marry. I would rather keep cats and a procession of scandalous lovers than end up in such a hotbed of silver loo and scandal one day because I forgot to live an exciting life.'

Marianne had to laugh at the highly unlikely scenario. 'I think perhaps you should become a playwright instead with an imagination like that,' she said.

'I really wish I had the talent for it, but was it really so awful living there?' Juno said as if she could not believe a lady so much older than she was could be bowed down by hard words and slights just as she was by those spiteful girls in London.

'Not really, I was feeling low and that colours the way you see a place, but it really was boring and full of bored people with nothing much to do but make up stories about anyone a little out of the ordinary to enliven their days.'

'I wish they would mind their own business, then.'

'So do I, but most of the time I barely heard the tutting and whispering about me. It was trying to pretend there was nothing wrong with me that made the world seem so bleak. Not being true to yourself is a curse I hope you never endure.'

'No, indeed, it sounds even worse than my miserably unsuccessful debut. So you hate Bath and I loathe London. I hope neither of us needs to set foot in them ever again, but there is not much hope of us ever being truly fashionable without one or the other of them to bring us up to scratch.'

'Perhaps we could endure it for some new clothes now and again and you could learn to endure the capital for a week or two to look suitably ravishing to enchant this beau you have been dreaming about meeting one day, I suppose? My mother has always insisted the London dressmakers are literally a cut above the rest.' Marianne thought Juno was trying to joke her out of her sadness and was touched. The girl had depth and character far beyond that of the usual debutantes and in a few years' time the polite world could be in for a shock when the Honourable Miss Defford finally came out of her shell.

'Not dressmakers, Mrs Turner, *modistes*,' Juno corrected primly. Marianne laughed at her imitation of a fine lady astonished anyone could even speak about such distinct branches of the craft in the same breath. 'And now there is Paris to outdo them all, since they say the finest modistes in the world live there and set the fashions everyone else is forever trying to catch up with,' Juno added.

'And what does Miss Defford say about Paris and all the finery she might find if only her uncle would consent to her going there?'

'That they are still only clothes and she is very happy as she is. I do not think I will care if I never see another fashion plate in my entire life.'

'Hmm,' Marianne mused. 'I expect you were always dressed in white as a debutante. With your dark hair and creamy skin you would look much better in colours and even

I love the luxury and fine texture of silks and good velvet as I move, as long as I do not have to wear them all the time and be forever worrying about getting dirty.'

'I cannot imagine you sitting in state all the time in order to keep your gown from harm,' Juno said with a rueful smile.

'No, neither can I,' Marianne said and shook her head at a fantasy of being Lady Stratford, dressed in silks and satins to please her lord and make her feel more of an aristocrat. That was a fantasy that could turn into a nightmare when it rubbed up against the day-to-day reality of trying to be someone she was not, so it was just as well it would never come true.

'You never did tell me how you know when a man is the right one for you, Marianne.' Juno interrupted her reverie, thank goodness, so she owed her another try at explaining the unexplainable.

'When he makes you forget any differences of rank and fortune and expectations between you. He may be a gallant fool who thinks he ought to put you first and walk away, even if it hurts you to even think about not being there to share his life with him from that moment on, but he is your fool nevertheless. Because he lights a fire in you that refuses to go out and maybe because he is uniquely himself. In the end it is simply because you love him and if he loves you back there is no better feeling on earth. Where he walks is where you want to go, too. Where he is going is the place you need to be.

'But although we were so certain we loved one another and it was right to have risked everything for him, there were days when I wished I had never met him, Juno. Sometimes I longed for safety and certainty and home when I was with Daniel in Portugal and Spain, but I would still rather have been with him than sit safely in Lisbon waiting for him to come back, or not. There were days when I wanted to weep with fatigue and hunger and Daniel wanted to send me away so I would not suffer the privations he had to endure so we could be together, but I am so glad I am a stubborn woman and I would not go, because that way we had so much more time together than we would have done if I was a biddable sort of person who does as she is told.'

'I will be sure I feel that much for a man before I risk everything for him then, but could a person love like that more than once, do you think?' Juno added so casually Marianne eyed her with suspicion. The girl could look so innocent she made lambs seem cynical.

'Maybe,' Marianne replied tightly and hoped that was enough to let Juno know there was some ground she should not tread on.

'I fear the poor old place has not been lived in for decades, Your Lordship.'

'I can see that for myself,' Alaric replied absently.

'It was a splendid old house in my grandfather's day. He often spoke of the fine company and days of feasting and dancing here when old Miss Hungerford was young and engaged to marry a baronet.'

'What happened?' Alaric asked, still staring at the uneven shamble of roofs added piecemeal when the owners wanted more room for guests or family and what looked like a long gallery tacked on to the roof of the west wing when fashion dictated every house with any pretensions to grandeur should have one.

'He ran off with a serving wench and was never heard of again. It was the scandal of the county and the locals swear Miss Hungerford's father caught up with the rogue, ran him through in a fury then buried his body so deep in the woods nobody will ever find him.'

'And the maid?'

'I suppose she ran away,' the lawyer said as if it had never occurred to him to worry about a servant girl. 'A runaway maid would soon find work in a city and it is not far to Gloucester or Hereford or even Bristol from here. The locals claim to see Sir Edwin walk on moonless nights searching for his lover, but I do not know how they expect anyone to believe it when such darkness stops you seeing your own hand an inch in front of your face, let alone the wraith of a man who probably got clean away, then lived out his life in disguise to avoid Miss Hungerford's father's wrath. I expect the maid got old and ugly and he regretted losing all this place must have offered a man for a pretty face and a comfortable armful.'

The lawyer was clearly not a believer in

the power of true love over rank and differences of fortune, even if he liked to tell an improbable tale. Alaric tried to block his ears to the man's chatter and assess the place as a possible home for himself and his family. Juno would like living anywhere that was not Stratford Park, its Dower House or Stratford House in London. And if only he could persuade her to marry him, would Marianne like this poor old place? She might relish the challenge of renewing and restoring an even more tumbledown house than her brother's equally ancient manor house was before she started. And yet... There was a forlorn air of old glories and future possibilities he felt guilty about turning his back on. If he ever managed to persuade the stubborn, challenging, extraordinary woman to let them both be happy, he would bring her here and let her make her own mind about it.

'Are there smugglers this far from the coast?' he asked as part of that story about ghosts walking rang true. Moonless nights would not betray signs the so-called Gentlemen were at work to the authorities, but they were a long way from the sea in this wild corner of Herefordshire nearly into the ancient mysteries of the Forest of Dean.

'The River Severn is tidal as far as Gloucester,' the man admitted cautiously so Alaric concluded he was right and the tale had been put about to keep the curious in bed on the darkest nights of the year.

'So an old tale of mayhem and haunting would be very useful to anyone with nefarious business in the dark,' he said, wondering if the house itself might be of use for storing cargoes since it was so forlorn and empty he doubted anyone had been employed to watch over it for a very long time. Smugglers to scout as well as spiders and vermin this time then, but if he could persuade Marianne to let them both be happy they could rid the poor old house of all its unwanted visitors and make it a perfect home for a hardworking country gentleman and his energetic lady.

'Indeed,' the lawyer said gloomily.

At least the man had fallen silent while Alaric worked through that reason for the old tale being embroidered and kept alive for such a purpose and they both brooded on the broken windows and tumbled slates of Prospect House as it sank into ruin. 'No,' Alaric said at last. 'I require a house and estate that needs hard work and dedication to get it all up to scratch and working well again, but this place has gone too far.'

It would not do to let the lawyer know he already felt angry the near-derelict old house had been allowed to get in such a state it was nearly too late to save it. He hoped to persuade Marianne to feel the same way about it as long as she would take him with it, of course. He could not live under the same roof as her one day longer and not let her and his niece and the rest of the world know he was in love with the woman. He had endured quite enough of being the honourable man and trying not to seduce his niece's companion was more than he could manage now he had spent three whole weeks riding about his native land pretending she was no more to him than any other ladylike companion for his niece might be and that he was not tortured by unsated need and yearning for her beside him in every bed he had slept in since the day he met her. She could either marry him or find another fool to drive to distraction with her stubborn temper and coolly challenging blue eyes.

He had borne weeks of it before he was wound up to such a pitch of wanting and needing her he knew he would break if he stayed with her and Juno on the road one day longer. For once it had been useful to be a lord with too many matters of business to neglect for much longer when he found an excuse to leave Juno with her and ride away. And at last that month was nearly up so she had best get ready to be thoroughly seduced by her former employer the moment he could bring that foolish contract to an end, if only she would finally admit they felt more for one another than a polite lord and Juno's companion should if they were to remain polite and companionly much longer.

'I will write to colleagues in nearby towns and see if they know of anything in the area,' the lawyer said with a last mournful look at the poor old house and a shrug as if he had done his best for it and it had been worth a try.

Luckily Alaric was looking for comfort and a house you could not lose half a regiment in without feeling crowded and this place could do very well. He was done with echoing glory and lonely staterooms; Stratford Park was far too uncomfortable and barnlike to live in day by day and he wanted far more from life than gilding and consequence and a marriage of convenience. This place was close enough to Owlet Manor to visit in a day and far enough away for them not to live in one another's pockets. And Chantry Old Hall was only twenty miles away as the crow flew, since crows could fly over water and that tidal River Severn was a significant barrier to humankind.

He suspected there was a lot more than employer and governess between Miss Yelverton and Harry Marbeck as well, but he would not lay odds on them reaching a happy ending. He sensed a troubled soul under Marbeck's determined pursuit of pleasure and deliberate provocation of the gossips, but if any female could tame him it was a Yelverton, so who knew? He was far more wrapped up in his own Yelverton female to even want to interfere and he hoped it was just a question of planning and hoping and not giving up on a very different dream than he thought he wanted before Juno went missing and his whole life seemed to collapse around him.

Chapter Seventeen

Marianne felt shaken and bewildered by the speed they had travelled since Juno received an invitation to spend a week or two with Miss Donne in Broadley and immediately wrote back accepting it and promising to be with her very shortly. The usually docile and obliging girl then insisted they travel as fast as they could go to get back to a place she had obviously been longing to be during this whole month of leisurely exploring this place and that.

So now here they were, back where they started. Marianne was not quite sure how she felt about being at Miss Donne's neat home where she had opened that lady's front door so unwarily that first memorable morning and found a travel-worn and exhausted viscount on the doorstep. Images of Alaric tense with exhaustion and worry and handsome as ten devils haunted her at the most inconvenient moments as it was. Being back in Broadley and visiting Owlet Manor without him when his presence there was imprinted on her memory as well would feel so bittersweet. He was hardly likely to come here when he knew Juno was safe and sound and happy with people she felt at ease with. Now he could go back to his old life and his fashionable and important friends and forget he had ever kissed a prickly woman who could not guard her tongue or her heart effectively whenever she was with him.

In a few months' time he would probably struggle to recall her name when they met to discuss Juno's next move and whether it was too soon to try and persuade his ward to try another London Season in the spring and hope for a much better outcome for her this time. Goodness, she was tired after all this travelling, though. She sighed and wondered what was wrong with her as she struggled to be glad Juno was so much happier now that her uncle obviously thought it was all right to leave her to carry on with her life without his constant presence.

Tiredness and a lack of spirits had dragged at Marianne ever since Alaric left them in Buxton. She looked back at the long days of work she had put into Owlet Manor before Darius married Fliss and sighed for the energy and single-minded verve of those first weeks and months at the dear old place, before life became complicated by love declared and fulfilled for her beloved brother and this unexpected and ridiculous love of hers for a man who probably did not want her anywhere near as much as she did him.

'Uncle Alaric!' Juno exclaimed as she stepped out of the hired carriage ahead of Marianne and ran towards her uncle like an eager schoolgirl.

And it was true! Lord Stratford really had just stepped out of the yard entrance to the Royal George at Broadley and now he was striding forward to greet his niece as if a magician conjured him up out of Marianne's yearning thoughts and what the devil was he doing here? Whatever it was she felt her heart race and colour flush into her cheeks as she wondered if she might be about to faint for the first time in her life. The shock of seeing him so unexpectedly made her feel light-headed and silly and then there was this urgent need to forget the rest of the world and run towards him and embrace him in such a very public place as soon as Juno had finished with him. The poor man would be horrified. Even the thought of his face as he fended her off with a harassed expression sobered her.

But, oh, dear, he was handsome, though, wasn't he? And strong and compelling as well and he made the rest of the world fade to silence and never mind the activity and noise all around them. She must be standing here gawping at him like an open-mouthed yokel. For a moment she dreamed of a fairy-tale world where they were the only ones who mattered to each other, until reality stepped back in and the rest of the world was suddenly noisy and curious and real again.

They were in a yard with horses and grooms and ostlers busy all around them and even the odd curious face or two at the windows looking to see what important personage had arrived this time in a luxurious carriage with outriders and mud-splashed and weary horses that said no expense had been spared in getting here as fast as possible. And Alaric was a lord and she was a lady's companion.

It was her own fault he had ordered himself to forget they had ever kissed one another as if they meant it, her doing. She had snapped and snarled at him so effectively he had treated her as an almost polite stranger from the moment they set out from Owlet Manor on this meandering journey to show Juno there was another world outside her schoolroom and the London ballrooms she had hated so much.

'Jojo!' he greeted the girl with a huge smile and a bear hug, then he swung her round as if she was light as a feather.

Marianne could not help but be impressed all over again by his strength, but why was he back in Broadley so soon when the *ton* must be on their way back to London to be brilliant and sophisticated and far more entertaining than they had time to be during the serious business of the spring Season and marrying off their daughters? Was he about to spirit Juno off to some elegant house party with his elegant friends and leave her here to wonder what to do next and mourn all the might-have-beens she could have had with him? She would miss the girl sorely and her new life as Juno's companion now she had come to know her so much better and value her as she deserved, but most of all she would miss him.

'Good day, my lord,' she said quietly as she stepped down from the post-chaise in her turn and tried not to feel breathless and elated at seeing him again. Her heart was beating so loudly in her ears she was surprised he could not hear it from where he was standing.

'Mrs Turner,' he said warily. She wished she could run into his arms, as sure of her welcome there as Juno had been, but there was no chance of that and she was seven and twenty and she did have her dignity to think about even if there had been. 'I trust you had a good journey,' he added as if he was very uncertain of his welcome as far as she was concerned and that hint of nervousness made her heart threaten to turn over with love for the annoying man right here on the cobbles of this busy inn yard.

'Very good, I thank you. The weather was most helpful for once,' she said stiffly instead of embarrassing him with a warmer greeting.

'Aye, the rain let up at exactly the right moment for the roads to dry up and be easily passable. Have you got everything you need out of the coach, Jojo? It seems best to keep moving so you two do not catch cold in this sharp wind, although the sun is being kind to us today. The luggage will be brought around to Miss Donne's house as soon as the horses are safely stabled.'

'Indeed, and you can trust the grooms to take even more care than usual with His Lordship's wrath to look forward to if they drop anything,' Marianne said.

'I can carry this bag myself,' Juno insisted.

Marianne was glad to see the stubborn set of her chin even if Lord Stratford eyed the small portmanteau as if he thought it looked too heavy for a lady to carry.

'If it means so much to have it with you, I will take it,' he insisted.

Marianne tried not to stare at the idea of a

lord spoiling the effect of his expensively elegant clothes, beautifully cut greatcoat and
fine beaver hat by carrying a rather femi-
nine-looking bag in the hand that was not
holding a gold-tipped cane she hoped he was
now only carrying for show. She frowned as
she looked back at him walking behind her
and Juno as a gentleman should. She tried to
see if he was still limping. If he was, then he
must have overstretched his ankle too soon.
She clicked her tongue in exasperation at his
headlong determination to push his body to
the limits, but he did seem to be moving
freely, if you discounted the bag Juno could
have had sent round later if she was not so
eager to bring presents back from her travels for Miss Donne and even brusque and
capable Bet.

'I cannot tell you how much I have missed
your glower of censure, Mrs Turner,' Alaric
told her with soft-voiced mockery, but did he
think Juno had gone deaf in the last couple
of weeks to tease her in front of his precious
niece?

'Well, I have not missed yours,' she parried sharply, but what a thumping great lie that was.

She was surprised when he looked almost hurt for a brief moment before he covered it with a cynical smile. Surely she imagined that instant of vulnerability in his blue eyes before he raised his eyebrows and nodded at something in front of her to remind her she needed to look where she was going instead of gazing back at him.

She had managed to forget how clear and compelling a blue his gaze was while they were apart, she realised as she marched ahead of him with her nose in the air and she did not need to look at him to know what he was like. His eyes were the same colour as the lapis lazuli used to paint the Virgin's gown in an Italian master's painting she saw years ago in a local magnate's house and had never forgotten. There was a depth of colour and such skill and love in that painting and she could have stared at it all day if only the house-keeper who showed Reverend Yelverton and his family around her master's splendid house and wondrous possessions allowed more than a snatched five minutes in each room.

Now she wanted to gaze into Alaric's deeply blue eyes even more than she had longed to stand and stare at that reverend, breathtaking painting all those years ago. He was so alive and subtly masculine and beautiful in his own unique way. Even with that bag in his hand a part of her wanted to stand and gape at him admiringly. Shock, she decided, as she tried hard to bring the rest of the world back into focus and think about that instead. Soon they would have covered the short distance between the posting inn and Miss Donne's little town house and she would have to have her wits about her when she met that lady's shrewd gaze again.

'Oh, my dears, how lovely to see you all again,' Miss Donne greeted them on her own doorstep. At least the door was open before Alaric could knock on it this time to save Marianne the sharp memory of how she had first met those blue, blue eyes of his with all the impatience in the world looking back at her and a pinch of desperation to give away the truth under his exhaustion and bluster. 'Now come on inside and stop letting all the heat out. There is a cold wind blowing today, for all the sun is shining to welcome you back to Broadley.'

'I will leave you to settle in,' Alaric said as soon as he had handed her precious bag over to his niece and he turned to go back to the inn where he must be staying. Marianne wanted to argue and tell him of course he must stay and she had missed the sight and sound of him for far too long for him to disappear as soon as they got here, but it was not her house and certainly not her place to bid him stay or go.

'We will see you for dinner then, Lord Stratford,' Miss Donne said as if they had arranged a timetable between them that Marianne and Juno had no idea about, but might as well go along with.

Marianne decided the lady was even more formidable than she had thought she could be when she chose and had obviously chosen to discuss arrangements for their visit in general and tonight in particular before Marianne and Juno got here.

'Dinner?' Juno mused after she bade a hasty farewell to her uncle and shut the door behind him after one last hug to say both of them were delighted to be together again, even if they were not staying under the same roof.

'A meal I take at a more fashionable hour than most of my neighbours since I got used to dining late with the great and the good during my years of employment as a governess, Juno, my dear. So I suggest we have tea and some of Bet's excellent scones to stave off the hunger pangs after your journey as soon as you and Mrs Turner have taken off your outer clothing and washed your hands.'

'Marianne, not Mrs Turner,' Juno corrected and Miss Donne seemed to weigh that familiarity up and decide that, as Juno was not a schoolgirl now, it would do between a young lady and her companion, but not for her.

'You must allow an older and more old-fashioned soul like me to keep one or two formalities alive, Juno. I suspect I am several years older than Mrs Turner's mother and doubt that lady would approve of such informality between us.'

'I dare say not, but she seemed very stuffy to me and what she does not know about cannot hurt her,' Juno said and followed

Marianne upstairs to the neat and sunny bed-chamber she had inherited from Fliss.

Marianne hoped dinner would be more formal than usual and that Miss Donne had invited her friends to eat with such a grand gentleman. That way she would be able to fade into the background and he would hardly notice she was there among so much flutter and curiosity. So she told herself she was disappointed when she came downstairs to find only four covers set out on the dining-room table and they were obviously going to have a quiet evening together where conversation would be unavoidable. There was a feel of cosy intimacy about the room with the fire lit and several branches of fine wax candles waiting to lend a glow to highly polished furniture and immaculate tableware. So there would be no avoiding Alaric's perceptive gaze with so few people to hide behind.

She was not sure if she was glad or sorry that she had put on the silk-velvet gown Fliss and Miss Donne made for her in the summer now. The beauty of the fine stuff and the way her friends had made it drape elegantly over her slender figure meant it was a delight to wear and it was warmer and more fashionable than any of her muslin or cambric gowns. But it clung to her a little too lovingly whenever she moved. Tonight was going to be difficult enough without adding sensual awareness of her every move to the mixture, but it was too late to change her mind now.

'Ah, there you are, my dear,' Miss Donne said as she bustled in to inspect the table and twitch a few items of cutlery this way and that. 'That is much better,' she said as if a quarter of an inch here and there had made any difference. 'Flowers are the final touch we need to make it perfect, I think. Could you see to that while I help Bet with the roast duck, Mrs Turner?' she requested with a vague gesture at the two fine vases on the pier table before she went out again.

Not relishing handling the beautiful little porcelain vessels or risking making a mark on the highly polished mahogany, Marianne lifted the finely made things very carefully. She dared not trust herself with them in the busy kitchen, but made her way out of the French doors Miss Donne had put in to get to her garden without going through the rest of the house. There was a welcome feeling of peace in the twilit garden, although she was very glad of the fine cashmere shawl Darius and Fliss had presented her with when she left Owlet Manor for her present position. She carefully put the vases down on the one bare deal table in Miss Donne's neat greenhouse and found the scissors the lady used for flowers easily enough. At least it had not rained for several days now, so her most delicate evening slippers would not get wet and be ruined.

Peering around the garden and trying to recall what was where from earlier in the year, she frowned and wondered how she was going to fill even those delicately exquisite little vases with flowers in early October. Luckily there were a few late blooms on Miss Donne's precious Bourbon and China roses and a spray or two of Michaelmas daisies. Finding some fine leaves just beginning to colour for autumn and a few sprays of rich red and orange berries Marianne began to relax and even hummed a tune to herself while she snipped stems to the right length and stripped off leaves and matched this against that until she was happy with the result. Yes, that would do nicely, she decided as she stood back to admire her handiwork. Just as well that she had neither flowers nor a vase in her hand when she finally realised Lord Stratford was watching her from the deepening shadows of the autumn garden, though.

'How you made me jump,' she accused him as he came to the doorway of the glasshouse as if he might as well admit he was here now and had been so for some time until she finally noticed him.

'At least an inch by my estimation,' he told her unrepentantly. 'You were so absorbed in your creations that half the peers in the House of Lords could have been parading through the flower beds and you would not have noticed them.'

'I think I might have,' she answered him with a smile and a chuckle for the picture he had put in her head of a troop of peers dressed in velvet and ermine and wearing their coronets as if for a state occasion as they filed through Miss Donne's precious garden in solemn but puzzled lines.

'I wish you would do that more often,' he said and because he had smiled back and come a lot closer she was not quite sure what they had been talking about any more.

'Arrange flowers?'

'No, laugh and hum under your breath and forget to be grave and responsible for a while.'

'I have to be, it is my job to be serious and take care of your niece.'

'Not with Miss Donne in the house and me to take my duty to Juno seriously for once in her life. Sometimes I see the bright, fearless and courageous girl you must have been when you met your Daniel under all that grief and responsibility you have learnt since, Mrs Turner, and I envy him like the devil.'

'He is dead,' she said bleakly and it did still feel bleak, even with this swirl of high excitement inside her making her breath come short and her heartbeat race like a mad March hare simply because Alaric was so close once again and she had missed him so very badly.

'I would never try to take him away from

you because I am jealous he knew the young and reckless girl you must have been back then and I did not,' he said in a low growl of a voice that told her he was being very serious indeed. 'You are who you are because you loved him and lost him before we met and I would not change that part of you even if I could.'

'You would not?'

'No, why would I want to, I…I…' His voice tailed off as if he recalled where they were and he was obviously uncertain how she felt about him. 'I like you very well as you are,' he substituted for the word her ears had been so eager to hear and never mind all those resolutions she had made while they were apart to treat him as her lordly employer and Juno's uncle in future.

'Like?' she still said recklessly.

'Definitely,' he said with a warm and almost lazy smile as he bent his head to kiss her as if he was tired of words and not quite being able to say what he really meant.

'I like you, too,' she echoed incoherently, then nuzzled closer to his firm mouth after snatching enough breath to go on with. Ah, this was what she had been missing so dearly it felt as if she was only going through the motions every day she had had to live without him. Now she was greedy for his kisses and his nearness and his l—whatever that was.

His mouth was warm on hers and his hands felt like heaven as he explored her curves through silk velvet. Even his finely made evening gloves only made his touch seem all the more fascinating through them and the silken caress of her gown with him on the other side of it. She wriggled a little closer and pouted kisses against his mouth to ask why he would not let her right inside and do the same for her. She heard his breath speed up, felt him tremble like a finely bred racehorse under her urgent, reckless touch and hoped he was satisfied to see that sensual Marianne was alive and very present after all. He was definitely not satisfied, she realised smugly as she slid her leg between his and felt how very far he was from that state for herself.

'Not here, Marianne, and probably not now,' he told her raggedly and tried hard to step back from her and the danger they would be very impolite indeed in Miss Donne's greenhouse if they did not put a little distance between them.

'When and where, then?' she insisted on asking wantonly as the little distance he had managed to put between them chilled her like midwinter.

'On our wedding night and in our own bed, if I have my way,' she thought she heard him murmur, but that had to be wrong.

Her mind was providing her with the words it wanted to hear out of her feverish need for him and his stubborn refusal to be less than noble about it, she told herself, as she stared up at him as if he had stuck a knife in her instead of maybe murmured something like a proposal of marriage. She shook her head to clear it of air dreams and nonsense. 'Now I am hearing things as well,' she muttered to herself as she felt him draw away and every part of her hated to let him go.

'Did I remember to dismiss you as of yesterday when you finally got here, Marianne?' he asked her huskily.

'Why? What have I done wrong?'

'Nothing yet and we did agree on a month's trial, did we not?'

'Yes, but…'

'But nothing, that month was up yesterday and never have thirty days seemed to tick by so wretchedly slow it felt as if every one of them was a month in its own right. So now you can consider yourself unemployed and free of any obligation to keep Juno company in future unless you do so out of the goodness of your heart, Mrs Turner.'

'I did not think I was doing so very badly at looking after your niece,' she said and now it was being taken from her she realised how much she had enjoyed getting to know the young woman she had spent so much time with lately and what on earth was she going to do with herself instead now she did not suit her noble employer?

'That has nothing to do with it,' he told her with a hunted look as if he was being asked to explain something very difficult indeed. 'Harry Marbeck is a gentleman,' he said at last and she could not hide a smile at his look of frustration as if even he knew he was being an idiot.

'So you told me when he brought my sister to Darius and Fliss's wedding.'

'Precisely and I believe I also told you he would not seduce a lady in his employment simply because he is one at heart, whatever the gossips say about him,' he said and at last she understood what he was trying so hard not to tell her and she had a struggle not to laugh. Or maybe even sing out loud, or jump up and down with glee because apparently he wanted to seduce her after all and she felt exactly the same way about him.

'Hence your abrupt termination of my employment, I suppose?' she said to help him out, although how on earth he thought he was going to be able to seduce her with Miss Donne as her fierce chaperone she had no idea, but her heart was still singing at the very idea.

'It has been a very long month.'

She looked a question at him and wondered about the potential for making love in a glasshouse. She glanced about at the scrubbed-out pots and tin labels and a few sleepy plants on the edge of an autumn sleep and above all so much glass to make them visible to anyone who cared to look out of an upstairs window or out of a back door and decided not; it was a highly unlikely trysting place. They would be far too obvious from the house and probably to one or two of Miss Donne's neighbours as well, if they realised what was going on down here and trooped up to their attics to peer down at a scandalous lord and a far-too-willing lady.

'And I am going to marry you,' he insisted as if primed for an argument and getting his best one in first.

'No, you are not,' she told him emphatically and backed away as if he had insulted her. 'No, no, no, you are most definitely not going to do anything of the sort, Viscount Stratford,' she added just in case he had not understood her the first time.

'No wedding, no bedding,' he drawled with knowledge of the fiery heat that was coursing through her like wildfire in his smile and probably in his eyes as well if only she could see them clearly enough in the rapidly falling dusk that made her worries about them being seen out here less relevant.

Drat the man, but he knew perfectly well what he had done to her and he probably only kissed her in the first place to remind her how he could set her senses alight with one intent look and as for an actual kiss... Well, his kisses ought to be classified as dangerous weapons. 'I am never going to marry you, my lord,' she told him with an emphatic shake of the head that would probably do terrible damage to the topknot of honey curls softened by a few cunningly escaped ringlets Bet had wound it into to go with the finery of Marianne's best velvet gown. 'You are who you are and I am who I am and I did not become pregnant during five years of marriage, so of course it would be too much of a risk to take with your vast possessions and title if you were to marry me.'

'You are a gentleman's daughter and the widow of a hero who died to preserve the liberty of his country, but I am only a man who had a title, riches and possessions landed on him at seventeen. I did nothing to deserve or win it all, it merely dropped into my lap. Juno running away made me look hard at what matters in life and she is one who does, but I soon realised you do even more, Marianne. Once I crashed at your feet like a fool and learned to see people as they really are

I woke up to all the possibilities of a love match with you and felt like a complete idiot for ever thinking a marriage of convenience with the new Mrs Yelverton would be enough for either her or me. You have taught me how to love and I am daring to hope I can teach you to love me back if I keep on telling you how dearly you matter to me and how mistaken you would be to turn your back on us simply for the sake of a boy we might or might not give birth to between us and a title I do not care about.'

'I doubt you were the shallow fool you painted yourself even before Juno ran away,' she protested with the glow of all that love in his words and the light in his dear eyes she could still see in the twilight and never mind colours or daylight. She wanted to stare back and give in and accept everything they could be to one another, if only she dared believe she could be this lucky twice in one lifetime and he really would not long for a son. 'And I do wish you would stop chastising yourself for past sins only you seem to worry about now,' she added, simply to stop herself eagerly saying yes to him and all that lovely promise for the future.

'Finished?' he asked and even in the gloom she could see he had raised his eyebrows at her, as if he had worked that out for himself.

'No, it is a ridiculous idea and we should both forget you ever mentioned it.'

'I certainly will not.'

'Then you should. I can forget you said it so we can be easy again together over tonight and you will thank me for it when you come to your senses.'

'I am not a boy, Marianne,' he told her with a fearsome frown and he clasped his hands together as if he was afraid he might have to shake her for pretending he was anything less than a set and determined adult if he did not. He certainly looked set and determined on getting his own way.

'I can tell,' she admitted with a half-smile for his gruffness and the strength of the warmth and affection that bound them together as well as this constant sizzle of attraction she had cursed from the very beginning of their acquaintance. Even as she longed to be in his arms again and agreeing to anything he wanted them to be if only he would make love to her, she made herself curse it some more and told herself she could walk away from him even now.

'Stop treating me as if I am an immature fool who does not know his own mind. I love you and I intend to marry you and nobody else.'

'You love me?' she asked and gaped up at him like a fool. Even as she gasped out that almost unthinkable question warmth ran through her like quicksilver and all the cold and lonely places Daniel left her when he died suddenly felt full of light and air again. He had said he cared about her and there was that stumble over the like word, but she had not dared to hope he actually loved her. She let the wonder of it lift her up and make her feel new again and met his gaze with all she felt for him in her own dazed eyes and never mind if they could see each other clearly or not in the ever-increasing darkness. She even stepped forward, ready to walk into his arms before she remembered why she could not and would not marry him. 'But I am *barren*,' she reminded them both bleakly as if he might not have taken all the implications of that sad fact in even now.

The empty feel of that stark word reminded her how it felt not to be with child month after month, year after year. She had longed for Daniel's child because she loved him so much it would have been wonderful to make a baby between them. He would have been a fine father as well, patient and full of fun, but stern when he had to be.

And his children would be growing up without him even now, Marianne, her sensible inner self reminded her.

They would have to live their whole lives with only vague memories of his strength and feeling secure and loved by their father and that would have been so very sad for them and for her as well. She still regretted the lack of a single one of them to say she and their father loved one another through thick and thin and that love would always live on in his children. With Alaric that lack would become monstrous because of all he had to pass on to a son and she could not endure even the thought of him coming to hate his childless marriage.

'I really and truly do not care, Marianne,' said Alaric Defford, Lord Stratford, with one of those mighty shrugs of his to say why on earth would he?

'I do, though,' she told him flatly and knew she was being unreasonable, but the memory of those miserable days when her courses returned relentlessly month after month was not easy to blot out of her mind and make her listen to reason.

'Why?'

'Because you have a title and great wealth and probably more than one fine estate to hand on to your eldest son,' she fudged because she did not want him to see the pain her childlessness had caused her during her marriage to Daniel, just as she used to guard Daniel from it at the time.

'Not good enough for me, Marianne. You must come up with a better reason to avoid me as a husband than that one. If I could be rid of my title, I would do it tomorrow. It bent me out of shape and made me look at life from the wrong side of the mirror and now it is standing between you and me. How could I even want a son of mine to be landed with something that could twist him into a man he should not be, Marianne? If there is no obscure Defford branch that fell away from the family tree many years ago to inherit my title and entailed land, then Juno's children can petition for it if they choose to. Best to let the whole vainglory die with me, but if they want it they are welcome.'

'You ought to be a father just for the joy of being one.'

'There are plenty of children out there in need of one. I thought on my way here that first time, before I had even met you, there are so many runaways without a frantic uncle on their tails desperate to see them safe and happy. We can adopt a few of them in time and offer sanctuary to more, but for now I would be content for it to be you and me and Juno until we can relax into love and be ready for our children to find us.'

'No. We are not going to be together, so how can they, my lord?' she said, almost more cross with herself for persisting in her doubts than she was with him for being high-handed.

'Now that is just plain selfish of you, Mrs

Turner. Think of all the urchins who will never have you for a mother and don't you pity them for having just me instead? I will make a poor fist of things without you to put me right—just look at the mistakes I made with Juno.'

'You really mean to do this, then? Are you sure it is not a scheme you thought up to make me feel better about marrying you since I probably cannot have children?'

'Of course I do—did you ever know me to sit on my hands and only think about doing something that was crying out to be done?'

'Well, no, but I have only known you for a while.'

'It only took me a day and a half to wake up and see you were the only woman I have ever met I truly want to spend the rest of my life with.'

'So you thought up your idea for adopting orphans on the way here and made up your mind you were going to marry me when you were lying in bed battered and bruised and out of your senses? It sounds like a fairy story to me.'

'Yes. I wanted you from the moment I first

set eyes on you, Marianne Turner, and at least landing on my head that day must have knocked some sense in because I know this is real and unique and true, even if you are being your usual stubborn and impatient self and are refusing to believe me.'

'And given how impatient you are...' She let her voice trail off suggestively, hoping it would suggest he got on with seducing her so she could find a way to persuade him being his mistress would be enough for her. Then maybe she could convince herself because hope was tugging away at her stubborn certainty she would not be enough for him as soon as the glow of loving passionately and even wildly wore off.

'I have been learning patience from the first moment I set eyes on you, so that fish won't bite,' he warned her with too much knowledge of what she had been planning in his mocking smile. 'I am a fully mature male, Mrs Turner, not a rampant boy to be led around by his cock.'

'As if I would and I hope you will never say such things in front of Juno.'

'Of course not and, before you ask, I will

not be so forthright in front of the children either. I shall save that for you, my stubborn and unruly lady.'

'I have not said I will marry you.'

'Not yet.'

'Not at all.'

'Not yet,' he insisted with such intent in his eyes she did not need to see the colour of them, just the glint of stubborn determination and rampant need in them even in the dark. The 'yes' he seemed to want so badly trembled on her lips.

'Can you actually see any flowers in all this gloom, Mrs Turner?' Miss Donne's voice called out to remind her the rest of the world was still turning.

'You can carry one of the vases as a punishment for distracting me when I ought to have been helping,' Marianne murmured with a secret sigh of relief.

'For you, my love, anything and please do not think you have put me off with your brusque orders and severe looks because I rather like them now I know how much spice and sensuality is hidden underneath them. This is only the beginning and I will convince you I will only ever marry you. Even if I have to camp out on Miss Donne's doorstep and make you a scandal and a hissing in the town until you agree to marry me just to make me go away, I will do it.'

He would as well, she decided with a smile for the picture he had painted her and the heady hope love might truly be enough for a viscount and a widow if they believed in it enough. 'We shall see' was all she said to let him know how tempted she was to simply give in and enjoy them for the rest of her life.

For the rest of the evening they both tried to behave like polite acquaintances and eat their dinner because Miss Donne and Bet had gone to so much trouble to welcome them home. She could not have said what they ate if the fate of nations depended on it, though.

'Goodnight, sweet princess,' Alaric whispered in her ear as Miss Donne ordered Marianne to show him out while she resolved some mythical crisis in the kitchen so they could whisper at her front door once again and what a matchmaker outwardly prim and proper Miss Donne really was.

'Go away, you annoying viscount, you,' she told him as the feel of his mouth so close to her ear sent shivers of sensuous anticipation through her and made her ravenous for more. He was going to kiss it, on Miss Donne's doorstep with glimmers of light all around the square to make them visible to her neighbours. Ah, no, he was not going to kiss her. Disappointment ran a race with that fire inside her and won. 'You ought to know better,' she told them both. His low rumble of laughter sent even more shivers of frustration and need through her and she glared at him this time.

'Ah, but I know best,' he murmured and kissed her hand instead of her cheek as she had been thinking he might. Apparently hands were every bit as sensitive as the soft skin near her ear could be, if only he would linger there instead.

'Someone will see us,' she hissed and might have snatched her hand away if it was not so comfortable in his large one that her fingers seemed to have entwined with his without the rest of her giving permission.

'They will have to find out I am in love

with you sooner or later, so why not now?' he said as if it was as simple as that and if only it was.

'Because nothing can come of it.'

'Do you call this nothing, Marianne?' he asked, suddenly very serious indeed as their eyes met in all that faint borrowed light from other people's lamps and lanterns. He held up their interlocked hands, brushed the index finger of his other hand over her overheated cheek that was still waiting for his kiss. His eyes held a challenge now as well as so much warmth that she could not even summon up a shiver for the whisper of winter to come behind the gentler autumn night.

'No, I call it impossible,' she said just as seriously and felt that chill after all.

'Where there is enough love there is no such thing as impossible. You should know that better than anyone, Mrs Turner,' he said with a hint of bitterness in his deep voice because she was giving him less than she had Daniel.

'And my late husband would tell you I am the most stubborn female he ever came across if he was able to. If you think my Daniel had an easy time of it with me either before or after I was his wife, you had best think again, Lord Stratford.'

'I envy him never knowing which way you might jump, not being able to expect anything but the unexpected from you, but most of all I envy him the faith and love you had in him when you set out to marry him and never mind any obstacles between you.'

'And it took me six months to admit I could not live without him and not miss what we might have been every day for the rest of our lives. I did not know then what I know now or it might have been a lot longer.'

'I will never expect you to forget him, Marianne,' he said gently, as if the news of that six months had soothed something raw inside him and made him feel better about the effort it was costing him to persuade her in his turn. 'I am jealous of him, I admit that, but I do not want to jostle him aside and demand all the love you have solely for me. You loved one another for five years, my darling. I honour him for the good life you two made together in circumstances that would have made most ladies run screaming for their mothers.'

'At least I can safely promise I will not do that,' she said and saw triumph glint back at her as she realised it had sounded like a promise for their future. 'No, that was only a perhaps. Stop trying to rush me.'

'As if I could when you must be the most stubborn and overprotective woman on earth,' he said rather sulkily. That glimpse of the boy he once was being just plain difficult because he could not get his way made her love him more instead of less.

She was in even more trouble now. So much of her longed to launch herself at him and revel in his lovemaking that a world of warmth and love and sensuality in his powerful arms felt tantalisingly close. Love meant putting your beloved's happiness first and however much he wanted her now, would he still do so as the years went past and all his roles demanded children to carry them on? And he should have a wife the world respected as his equal, not a vicar's daughter who had managed to marry beneath her before she netted herself a viscount.

'You must know I have feelings for you. I do not see how you could escape knowing it when I virtually threw myself at you earlier this evening, but I am about as unsuitable a viscountess as you could find.'

'You have obviously not looked hard enough, then. You are a respectable widow, love, not a housemaid or a courtesan. We lords and even the odd duke here and there have always married women the world thought we should not and yet the world keeps turning and the aristocracy is still in its accustomed place and love is all that matters in the end.'

'Maybe, but we can stand here arguing black is white all night long and you still will not convince me I am viscountess material, my lord. Now kindly go away and let me go to bed. You have obviously been here for days winning over my friends and laying all sorts of devious plans for my undoing, but I have had a long journey and I am weary from it and about to lose my temper.'

'Heaven forbid,' he said with such a rueful smile inviting her to laugh that she felt her heart melting another degree.

'Go away,' she demanded and turned her head away to hide the answering smile that might give her away as a lot less certain she wanted him to than she had managed to sound.

'For now,' he answered and used their entwined hands to pull her much closer and snatch an unguarded kiss from her lips almost out here in the street.

It was so brief and hot and unsatisfying that she pouted and shot him a look of reproach, but he just grinned a wildcat grin, raised his hat in a mocking salute and walked away from her with that confounded cane of his swinging triumphantly at his side to say he was rather proud of his evening's work, never mind her 'no' and 'maybes'. And he had every right to be, she conceded with the heat and sting of not enough kisses still on her sulky lips. Oh, drat the man, how the devil did he expect her to sleep a wink tonight with all this hot wanting and doubt and fascination for him and his magnificent body and uniquely handsome face and all the things about him that made her love him churning about in her head?

Chapter Eighteen

'So what do you think of the poor old place, Marianne?' For once Alaric sounded uncertain, as if a lot more depended on her answer than it ought to.

'Someone should be very ashamed at the state of it. Even my Great-Uncle Hubert kept the roof repaired and windows mended, although that was about all he did do when he was master of Owlet Manor for the last fifty years of his life.'

'I know it is in a very poor state, but roofs can be mended and windows replaced. Could you live here, do you think?'

'Is any of it habitable?' she said suspiciously, because they had only set out on a drive today and he was even more devious than she thought he was now he was presenting her with a potential home rather than a picturesque view.

'That depends on how high your standards are,' he said evasively.

Marianne could tell he had fallen in love with the place since he had evaded her perfectly sensible question. She looked down at the derelict old house and the wild wood that had grown up around it since a gardener last came anywhere near the place. It was the perfect site for a manor house, just large enough to be a comfortable family home, if only it had a comfortable family living in it. What it could be, whispered a plea for someone to rescue it from ruin. The man was cunning, though, presenting her with a challenge like this one. With splendid views across the Severn Plain from up here and the sheltering hollow where the house was set out of the worst of the winds that would whistle up the Bristol Channel, she would need a heart of stone not to be tempted by its forlorn air of waiting for them to make things right again.

'I think we can safely say my standards are not high after some of the billets Daniel and I endured on the march, but what about you, my lord? Could you put up with the howling draughts and leaking roofs there must be in such a place while the builders repaired and redesigned the place for modern living around you, or would you visit the place occasionally until all the work was done and live in splendour at Stratford Park?'

'I would hire a house with proper windows and a roof nearby and be comfortable while I kept an eye on those builders and made sure it was all done as we wanted it. You would not have me leave them to it, would you?'

'No,' she said carefully, knowing he was expecting her to demand her say in how it would all be done and not quite ready to fall into his trap just yet. 'But why do you even want another house? Don't you have enough already?'

'I have more than I know what to do with, but this one would be yours. I know you secretly long for a home from some of the things Juno has said in her letters and my own incredible powers of observation. I want you to have one where only you can say who goes and stays and what is repaired and what replaced. I admit that I came here looking for a home where Juno could be happy if you washed your hands of both of us and walked away, but I knew as soon as I saw it that this place should be yours and somehow I would have to persuade you to let me share it with you. And if anything ever happens to me I want you to have a home that will always be yours to do with as you please.'

'Why would anything happen to you, Alaric? And how do you think I could endure living here without you? People make homes, not stones and timbers and leaky roofs.'

'My brother died when he was five and twenty, so I know I cannot promise I will live until I am ninety and die at the same moment you do, Marianne, but I have no intention of going anywhere without you if I can help it.'

'Good,' she said and her heart missed a beat as she thought about the uncertainty of life and he was right, it was all a risk, but so few things in life that were worth having came without a bundle of those. She loved him so fiercely and truly and did not want him to think he had won her over with a house. It was important he would always know that he came before any of the riches and wonders he could shower on her and Juno and any other family they managed to make along the way. 'You have fallen in love with this poor old house, haven't you?' she said suspiciously.

And there was his shamefaced look he wore when he was trying to hide his deepest feelings and at least she recognised it now. She hid a smile when he decided they needed to take a closer look at the place to disguise his discomfort at being found out so easily. She was very glad of the warm rugs over their knees and the not-quite-so-hot brick at her feet he had provided to keep the chilly autumn air at bay as best he could.

He had surprised her by driving up to Miss Donne's house this morning in his beautifully sprung curricle and demanding her company and please to hurry before his precious pair of perfectly matched Welsh greys caught a cold. Now Alaric looped the long tail of his driving whip neatly after giving the high-stepping pair the signal to risk the first part of the drive to this forlorn old house so she could take a closer look.

'It needs someone to love it before it falls down,' he finally admitted when the ruts in the overgrown lane made it criminal to risk his horses' legs further by trying to get even closer, so he halted them again.

'It might take a lot of effort to keep on loving it at times,' she cautioned. 'Most people you ask to come and repair it will advise you to have it pulled down and build something modern and convenient in its place.'

'Would you?'

'No, but I must be as totty-headed as you are because I would rather restore it and add a few modern touches to make it easier to live in.'

'Such as?'

'I need to see more before I am able to tell you that.'

'Then we might as well go in and take a look,' he said and heaved a vast bundle of huge keys out of the boot as the tiger shook out the rugs that had been folded up in there to cover the horses. 'Walk them for me to save them from a chill, will you, Portman?' he asked the wizened little man who had not said a word in Marianne's hearing all the way here and just nodded and went to croon at his precious horses now.

'You have already bought this sad old house, have you not?' Marianne asked when Alaric offered her his free arm, since the other one was fully occupied with that ring full of ancient and heavy-looking keys.

'I thought it would make a fine place for our orphans,' he admitted with a slightly hunted look as she gave him a sceptical look, but still took his arm, because there were so many potholes in the unkempt drive it would have been foolish not to.

'Your orphans,' she corrected him nevertheless.

'Don't you like the idea of them learning to be happy here and growing up in the fresh air and sunshine?'

'Of course I do. I am not sure what the locals will think if they are unruly as some of the children who used to trail along with the army on the march.'

'There you are, you see, I shall need you to keep order.'

'I doubt it, Lord Stratford,' she told him severely, but she was warming to the scheme he seemed so set on carrying out whether she agreed to marry him or not and he knew it. 'Now stop prevaricating and let me see inside.'

'It is very bad,' Alaric admitted half an hour later and even he looked doubtful now. 'Perhaps those builders you told me about earlier are right. It could be better to pull it down and begin again.'

'I think the kitchen will have to be rebuilt before any self-respecting cook will agree to cook as much as an egg in there and you are right—and the east wing is beyond repair, but the rest seems possible. There are even more cobwebs and several tons more dust in here than there were at Owlet Manor when I got there, but most of the timbers seem sound and even where the rain has got in they can be renewed or replaced once the roof is mended.'

'And there are details it would be a shame to throw away, like the grand staircase and all this fine oak panelling. I am not sure I want to sleep in a state bed as vast as the one in the best bedchamber—I might lose you of a night.'

'You have not got me to lose yet,' she reminded him, but she was weakening and had just gone another step closer to giving in. She could feel him being a little bit smug and a lot more impatient again for her final 'yes' to Lord and Lady Stratford and their tumbledown old folly of a house.

'There is all the world yet to gain then,' he said with a pretend sigh. 'How I wish there was even one room here clean enough to seduce you in and bend you to my wicked ways with hot kisses and a great deal more,' he said with a serious question in his wary expression as he looked down at her this time.

'So do I,' she answered it quite seriously.

'And your brother has finally taken his wife on a bride journey, now all his crops are in and they have a new farm manager in place to make sure there is at least some cider left when they come home.'

'So he has,' Marianne said dreamily.

'And I have wanted to find out how far this place is from Owlet Manor ever since I first discovered it so that you will not feel cut off from your family when we live here.'

'Do not push your luck, my lord.'

'But, of course, there is the problem that without the prospect of a wedding there can be no bedding for us,' he said virtuously.

'You know how much you want me,' she said and it was not vain of her to point that fact out, it was purely practical. She was so deep in love and longing and needing him now it felt like a fever in her blood.

'I do, but I also know how much you want me, Mrs Turner.'

'Do not remind me,' she murmured and tried to blank out the gnaw of frustrated need burning at the centre of her that was threatening to become a wildfire blown out of control as he stared back at her with one of his own in his brilliantly blue eyes.

'I will use any means I can to persuade you into my bed and my arms and my life for good, Marianne. Otherwise we will both have to burn and we know whose fault that is. I might run mad and look what you will have done then.'

'I...' Marianne let her voice tail off because

she could not think of any reason strong enough to keep this raging need at bay any longer. The burn of unsated need deep within her and the sting of wanting and not having was sapping her rational mind and he had already turned her set-in-stone determination not to marry him into a whole flock of 'maybes' and 'yes, I will.' 'I am burning, I am so hungry for you I cannot lie about it any longer and you are right and I do love you, Alaric. But how can we make it for good when we are so very different in so many ways?'

'Because love matters and wherever and whenever it comes along it should not be ignored and pushed aside. You loved Sergeant Daniel Turner so finely and recklessly and so well, why would you make a second love with me into something less, Marianne? I honour the man for having the sense to love you so completely, but you two were supposed to be divided by birth and education and goodness knows how many other barriers, but you demolished them all between you. Am I so much less of a man you will not do the same for love of me?'

There was all the doubt he was a good man with a true heart in his eyes now and it was her fault. She had met the real man under the title when he was laid low by his head injury and still stinging from Juno's rejection. And now he had Marianne Yelverton-Turner to make him feel unwanted and uncertain of his many and far-too-plentiful attractions, he did not need his mother to reject and belittle him, did he? She hated herself for putting those doubts back in his clear blue gaze again and found her courage at long last.

'No, you are a wonderful man, Alaric. Strong, loving and true and your brother would be so proud of the man you are now, but how can I ever live up to your high standards if I agree to marry you?'

'If you ask me, the boot is on the other foot.'

'I do love you,' she admitted, 'and it has nothing to do with this poor forlorn old house before you get carried away by the idea I would only agree to marry you to get my hands on it. I wanted you from the instant I met your bloodshot eyes through the gap in Miss Donne's door. I knew I would have to want the instant I found out who you really were, but that did not mean you were not the unshaven pirate baron who stole my heart when I thought I did not even have one left to steal.'

'And I wanted you just as instantly, my fierce Mrs Turner, and never mind the exhaustion dragging at my heels and the driving need to find Juno and make sure she was safe. I did not know you liked unshaven pirates, by the way. I shall have to work a lot harder on some sea-dog ways.'

'Please do not. I doubt the world could cope with you rampaging around it, stealing cargoes and kidnapping lady pirates to carry off to your lair.'

'My, you do have an exotic imagination.'

'I do,' she told him with a silly, besotted smile as a good many of her fantasies offering a future of wild lovemaking could be hers if only she could reach out and grasp it and forget all her doubts that it was the right thing to do. 'What if you regret me in a few years' time, Alaric?' she asked very seriously as she pushed those tempting scenarios aside for a maybe later.

'Did you ask Turner that when you packed your bag and stole out of your father's vicarage with the dawn to find him and marry him, Marianne?'

'No.'

'Then why are you asking me to put a limit on my love for you? I will still love and need and desire you when I am in my dotage. Right now I am not quite sure which will come first, having you in my life and finally admitting we cannot live without one another or reaching my dotage before you will finally say "yes" to me.'

'I am ready to right now,' she told him, certainty that he was right exploding all her scruples at last. 'I love you so much I have to believe we can cross off all the items on my list of why we should not marry, Alaric. I will love you until my dying day.'

'Then will you marry me?' he said and got down on both his knees, on this filthy floor inside this broken-down old house. 'I love you beyond words and promises, Marianne, but please will you help me to remake Viscount Stratford and be my love and my wife as long as we both shall live?'

'You had better do a lot of it, then,' she told him acerbically. 'I am not losing another love for life and having to spend mine without you, so you had better make up your mind to living with me for a very long time, Alaric, Lord Stratford.'

'Is that a "yes"?' he asked her, a world of hopes and dreams naked in his eyes along with a full measure of lust and a side dish of fantasy to add to the mix.

'Of course it is, you silly viscount. Now will you finally get up and kiss me properly before I faint from pure need on this very dirty floor.'

'Not yet,' he replied tensely as he got to his feet and stood a frustrating few yards away from her.

'Why not?'

'Because I am not stopping once I have started and we have already established there is nowhere in this poor old wreck of a house fit for us to make love for the first time in the very long love affair we are about to begin.'

'How fast can those horses of yours go, Alaric?' she asked with a world of hot need opening out in front of her and an urgent desire for everything she had fantasised about him coming true as soon as they could get to a clean house with a clean bed in it.

'Since I will not have you slammed about and bruised as we tear around corners and bounce over potholes, you are not about to find out.'

'Then perhaps an inn…?' She let her voice trail off as the suggestion lit even more fires in his already hot-blue gaze. 'Your tiger would know what we were about, of course, but I really am beyond caring. I want you so much, Alaric.'

'And do you really think he is going to tell anyone? The man only speaks to horses with the occasional grunt for me if he is in a particularly good mood.'

'He does seem taciturn.'

'He is and, even if he was the best gossip in England, I do not care who knows I love you to the edge of reason and I cannot keep my hands off you for very much longer.'

'Well, that is very good news as far as I am concerned since I feel the same way about you, but fine words butter no parsnips, my lord. Action is what is needed right now.'

'I agree,' he said and they could hardly fumble the ancient great lock on the front door back into place fast enough before they joined hands and ran carefully down the wild grass at the side of the drive because they might be in love and desperate to prove it to one another, but Lord Stratford had spent enough time laid up with damaged limbs and a broken head lately.

Chapter Nineteen

They did manage to contain themselves by maintaining a tight-lipped silence all the way back to Owlet Manor, but by the time they got there they were very glad to hand the curricle and horses over to the uncommunicative little man who had been sitting up behind them for miles frowning over their heads at his precious horses.

'Hurry,' Marianne urged Alaric when he would have stopped to say something polite and gentlemanly to Fliss's new housemaids.

'Now they will gossip,' he said as they ran up the familiar stairs to the quaint old bedchamber Marianne had fallen in love with on her first day at Owlet Manor. It seemed fitting that the first place that had felt like home since she left her father's old vicarage would be the place where she first made love to her future lord and true lover.

'Let them, I do not care,' she gasped, tugging him in through the door of the room as she took a quick look around it in the fast fading light and realised Fliss had not changed a thing in here. It did still feel hers and she hoped Fliss would forgive her for this intrusion into her new domain. Marianne rather thought she would once she had explained there were no convenient shepherd's huts on their way here and this was her first time with the man she loved, so it deserved to be private as well as special from one end to the other.

'I do not expect you to love your Daniel less because you love me as well, Marianne,' Alaric managed to tell her huskily despite the frantic need she had sensed him barely holding under control for miles as he drove with almost too much care so he did not take unnecessary risks with her safety.

'Thank you,' she said sincerely and put her cold fingers against his even colder face and held them there to warm them both and because she did love him so much she wanted

to touch him and warm him and show him
how lovable he really was and how very, very
strong and manly and kind and—

Just get on with it, Marianne; love the man
before you both faint from frustration.

'But love is generous, my darling, so there
is enough of it in my heart for both of you
and I shall never love *you* less because I love
him as well.'

'I am not sure I can give you gentle, though,
and you deserve it,' he told her unsteadily.

'Do not put curbs on us, Alaric. However
much you try to reason it into a corner and
control it we want each other quite shamelessly.'

'That does not mean we cannot have tenderness as well as passion,' he said stubbornly and covered her hands where they still
cupped his face and stared down into her
eyes with his loving, lingering touch against
her skin. 'Love,' he said with wonder still in
his eyes.

'Yes.'

'I want you so much my eyes are cross-
ing,' he told her and she stood on tiptoes for
a closer look and nodded sagely at him to say

so they were and the closer she looked the more hers were as well.

'Time to stop talking, then,' she said practically and raised her mouth for his kiss and to get him to give her the use of her hands back, so she could touch and hold and encourage him as he did the same for her. It was the lovely loving connection of it all that made her gasp and her body sing as they fell on one another with a hunger that had been too long building to be slow or carefully seductive now. Fire and fierce passion and that streak of tenderness under it all that he had promised them seemed to draw something wondrous out of them as they fell on each other and reached higher and faster than it felt they had ever been before. She fell back to earth with a sob for the loss of that ecstatic, languorous place they had just claimed as their own for the first time. It was the lovely, fiery, intimate connection of it all that thrummed through them like a force of nature as they lay together in the bed they had finally found the strength to climb into and count their racing heartbeats back to earth as breath came softer and kisses even more honeyed.

* * *

'Oh, goodness!' Viola gasped as she caught the wedding bouquet Marianne cunningly aimed at her almost by accident. Viola stared down at the posy of white camellias and dried lavender flowers and dark green and fragrant myrtle leaves. 'Typical of you two,' she said as she sniffed the herbs and stroked the velvety petals and refused to blush at the speculation in their mother's eyes.

'What? A mix of homespun and exotic?' Marianne said as she met Alaric's eyes and forgot what they were talking about at the leap of masculine interest in there for that intriguing idea. *Pirate Alaric*, she mouthed with an encouraging smile.

'No, an ideal combination for a Christmas wedding,' and Viola's voice reminded Marianne this was a doubly serious occasion with a roll of her eyes at their ridiculous preoccupation with one another.

'Or any other time of year,' Alaric told his bride of a few minutes and kissed her as if he could not help himself now they had got started on loving one another for life.

'Stop it, you two, and kindly get inside that

fine carriage and let yourselves be driven up to the house so the rest of us can get warm again,' Darius told them gruffly from his place just behind the bride and groom with Fliss at his side trying not to laugh at him for playing gruff lord of the manor.

'Take no notice of him,' Fliss advised the newly married couple. 'Having a viscount in the family seems to have gone to his head.'

'Hmm, he is not the only one, then,' Viola murmured as the sound of Mrs Yelverton condescending to Miss Donne even more than usual reached them even at the church door.

What might have spoiled a lesser day passed Marianne by on this very special one and she thought Miss Donne could cope with far sterner foes than the proud mother of the bride. With Alaric's strong hand in hers and his almost boyish delight in their simple country wedding, even her mother's love of a title seemed amusing rather than embarrassing, today anyway. So she ran out to the waiting carriage at Alaric's side and was glad when it was on its way because once they were out of it and inside it could go back for her father so that he could be got out of the cold as soon as possible and hopefully breathe more easily in the seat by the fire Fliss had saved for him.

'I love you, Husband,' Marianne said with an infatuated sigh. She had to love him even more for taking such care to get her father here by even shorter stages than last time so he would not get quite so cold and might not wheeze so badly in the damp December air.

'And I love you, Lady Stratford.'

'Let's not talk about her today, I am too happy to worry about high and mighty peeresses like her right now.'

'You are one all the same and I still love you.'

'Best not adore me too much, Alaric, I might become an idol and develop feet of clay.'

'Remind me to make a list of all your faults and read them out to you once a month then—that ought to keep you humble.'

'If you like the feel of sleeping in an empty bed each night of it, then you go right ahead and do so, my lord.'

'That I do not. It was far too empty while

you were making up your mind whether to love me or not for me to risk that much loneliness ever again.'

'I had no choice but loving you when it came down to it. I could not forget you from the moment I first set eyes on you.'

'Ah, yes, pirates—I wonder if my valet has remembered to pack my cutlass.'

'The poor man would give in his notice if you asked him for one of those and you are more likely to need a hammer and chisel where we are going.'

'It will not be a very romantic place to spend our honeymoon,' Alaric said almost as if he regretted the leisurely journey to somewhere more exotic they could have had when they were about to move into the hastily refurbished Agent's House at Prospect Manor instead.

'I think it will be the perfect place for one,' Marianne said with the busyness and bustle they would stir up there making it seem the ideal way to spend the first days of their marriage. 'Far better than us flitting about from mansion to mansion as you introduce me to your friends and neighbours. I doubt they will want to know me and I am not looking forward to meeting them.'

'Stop it, love, you are as good as any of them and better than a good many.'

Seeing it really did disturb him to hear her worry what his friends would think of her, she tried to push her anxiety aside. No, it would not do. 'We cannot keep our worries quiet from one another, Alaric. We must learn to share them so they do not push us apart.'

'Very well, then, as soon as I manage to convince you I have the finest and most desirable viscountess in the land we shall take a tour of my lordly obligations and show everyone why I insisted on marrying you despite your dogged opposition to the idea. It will not help Juno realise there are good people at every level of our society if you refuse to believe it yourself.'

'I did not think of that,' Marianne said with a frown. 'I suppose I must learn to act the great lady after all, then.'

'No need to act, you are one already. I know our tenants and neighbours will breathe a sigh of relief and welcome you with open arms after so many decades of regal indifference to their needs and hopes from my mother.'

'She has a lot to answer for,' Marianne said sternly as the carriage reached the front door of Owlet Manor only moments after it set out from the church.

'Never mind her now, this is the best day of my life so far and I am not going to spoil it by picking over old griefs and sorrows. Yours are different.'

'You mean Daniel?'

'Of course.'

'If there was a way of doing it, he would dance at our wedding today, Alaric. He truly loved me and would have hated to see me so haunted and miserable and grief-stricken as I was for so long after I got back to England and until the day I met you, if I am being strictly truthful. You are the very man he would have picked out for me because you are the best man I have ever met apart from him. I will never forget him, but that does not mean I cannot love you every bit as much as I loved him.'

Marianne felt as if this conversation was even more important than the vows they had made one another in front of God and their nearest and dearest, if that was possible. 'I love you so much, Alaric. I thought it was impossible for a woman to be lucky enough to love with all her heart twice in one lifetime, but you have proved to me how wrong I was.'

'You have all of my heart, Marianne. I never thought I could love like this at all, so just look what you have taught me,' Alaric said and they kissed under the ball of mistletoe and bright ribbons the servants must have placed there once the wedding party set out for the tiny church. Breathless and excited and looking forward to loving this man in every sense of the word once again and as soon as they could get some privacy and a bed to celebrate it in, Marianne felt the earth spin under her feet and the stars shift in their spheres. Alaric kissed her with such passion she wondered if it was possible to be driven out of your senses by love and desire and they could have been anywhere, at any time of year, for all she could feel of the lazy December wind and an overcast sky that said there might be snow in it somewhere or more probably rain what with this being England

and the weather likely to change from hour to hour.

'Oh, for goodness' sake,' Darius interrupted them who knew how many minutes later as the next carriage rumbled up to the door and swept around the newly laid carriage sweep with a flourish. 'At least get inside out of the cold so we can get on with the Christmas feast you have promised us, Stratford. My sister will take to her bed with the influenza instead of the reason you want her there if you do not stop kissing one another soon and get inside.'

'Very well, Papa,' Marianne said mockingly and was astonished to see her brother blush for the first time since they were children. 'You are not, are you?' she asked him and when he only stood there on his own carriage sweep looking like a boy caught out in mischief she looked to Fliss for an answer instead.

'I told him it was to be our secret until after today, but sometimes he is such a boy I cannot rely on him to keep a still tongue in his head,' her sister-in-law scolded her large and mature husband and Marianne could see him turning to mush in front of her eyes. He was going to be such a wonderful father and if this happened to be a little girl she could just imagine him being wound around her little finger the second she was born.

'But that is such wonderful news you should not have kept it quiet for our sake.'

'No, this is your day. We had ours… um…' Fliss stopped as if remembering a bit too much of that night when she and Darius first made love up in the hills the day Juno went missing and shortly before Lord Stratford knocked at Miss Donne's door and demanded to see Fliss. 'In August,' Fliss finished bravely, although it remained to be seen if their babe might give away exactly when that day was or if he or she arrived a tactful nine months after Fliss and Darius's wedding.

'I am so pleased for you both,' Marianne said and truly meant it. She felt Alaric's anxiety for her hearing such news when they were never likely to have their own child as he wrapped a strong arm round her waist and pulled her closer. 'I have all I want right here,' she told him softly and forgot family and guests all over again. 'And there are those runaways and urchins to look forward to taking in if you truly do not mind your title going to waste one day.'

'Good riddance to it,' he said and kissed her again because it was a shame to waste a good kissing bough.

'You will wear it out,' Darius said with a push to get them inside and out of the cold at long last, then he made thorough use of it himself before pulling a blushing, laughing, flustered Fliss inside after him so they could make way for more soberly happy wedding guests who eyed the kissing bough with either suspicion or nostalgia, then sped inside unkissed rather than risk getting cold.

'Your brother is a rogue,' Alaric told Marianne between welcoming their guests and at least Mrs Yelverton was too much in awe of him to try and push her way in front of him as she had with Fliss and Darius at their wedding.

'I know, but Juno would never have come to Broadley if she was not looking for Fliss and I would never have discovered you unkempt and arrogant on the doorstep this summer. So we owe one another to Fliss, if not my brother.'

'Then he can say what he likes since I never want to imagine my life without you in it ever again,' he murmured between handshakes and smiles for these people they loved enough to invite to their very select wedding.

'Neither do I,' Marianne agreed and once again Lord and Lady Stratford proved what an unconventional pair they were by kissing one another in full view of their guests as if they could not help themselves and they really could not so they kept on doing it until the bride's brother ordered them into the dining room and made them sit on opposite sides of the groaning table in order to make them at least pay lip service to the proprieties.

'What a scandalous couple we are, love,' Alaric told her across all the pies and roast this and that and enough left over to feed everyone for miles around, just as he intended when he sent for it all.

'I love you,' she replied, 'so much that it probably is scandalous, but I don't care.'

'Nor me,' he said and after that the wedding breakfast of my Lord and Lady Stratford had to manage without them, so it was just as well most of their guests were more amused than offended by the scant attention they paid to their own nuptial feast.

'Wedding breakfast in bed, now there's a novelty,' Alaric told his wife some time later when he brought in the tray Fliss had ordered left outside their room until they were hungry, if still not feeling very sociable.

'I love experiencing new things since I met you,' Marianne told him with a siren smile and they made a very stimulating meal of it, eventually.

* * * * *

LET'S TALK
Romance

For exclusive extracts, competitions
and special offers, find us online: